The Secret Life of the Panda

The Secret Life of the Panda

Nick Jackson

Chômu Press

The Secret Life of the Panda

by Nick Jackson

Published by Chômu Press, MMXI

The Secret Life of the Panda copyright © Nick Jackson 2011

The right of Nick Jackson to be identified as Author of this
Work has been asserted by him in accordance with the
Copyright, Designs and Patents Act 1988.

Published in December 2011 by Chômu Press.
by arrangement with the author.
All rights reserved by the author.

ISBN: 978-1-907681-13-4

First Edition

Design and layout by: Bigeyebrow and Chômu Press
Cover artwork by: Suzanne Norris

E-mail: info@chomupress.com
Internet: chomupress.com

"Every man is an abyss, and you get dizzy looking into it." – Woyzeck

Georg Büchner

Contents

Anton's Discovery

The bird beat its wings against the walls of the trap Anton had set. He felt the ribs crack as he reached in to grasp it. His heart was pounding and he was light-headed just to be holding it—this elusive creature, so familiar and yet unreachable. Now he had it in his hand. The feathers brushed against his skin and the scrabbling feet pricked his fingers. The bird's beak jabbed—once, twice—at his palm and drew blood and it turned its head to look at him with its button-black eye. He felt the throb of its body and marvelled at the strength of a thing so small. Then, quite abruptly, it gave a shudder and became a limp corpse in his hand. He was so shocked he dropped it.

Anton looked round then to see if anyone had seen what he'd done. The windows of the house were empty. The servants were rattling pans and brushes in the kitchen but no one was looking out and the garden was deserted.

He squatted down to look at the bird's body. The eyes were clouded with a faint grey-white sheen; just moments before they had glared up at him. Now, because of him, they were glazing over. The beak that had attacked his hand was lifeless; he noticed a single bead of dark blood oozing out. Again he looked round to see if he was alone. It occurred to him that he should bury it, but he had no shovel. He thought of scraping out a hollow with his hands and burying it amongst the weeds. Then he felt a pang at the thought of the glossy feathers covered in soil, the eyes coated with grit and dust.

Finally he lifted it up and gently pushed it under the fern fronds. Only the feet, the yellow grasping claws, were visible, and he hid them with a piece of moss.

Gradually he became aware that his mother's voice was calling him.

"What have you been doing, Anton?" she asked, as he passed her on the stairs.

"Nothing. I was in the garden."

"Look at the state of your clothes! Come here. How did you get in such a mess?"

From the way she looked at him, he thought she must have seen what he had done but she only said: "Your father wants you." She was breathless from reaching to clean a window ledge. Her hands clutched the cloth, wringing the wetness from it.

"I'm going there now," he said.

But he didn't go to his father's room. He shut himself in his own room and thought of the corpse outside in the garden under the ferns. It would have been better to bury it. There was a knock at his door and his sister Johanna put her head round with that look she had, the formal pursing of the lips she copied from her mother.

"Father wants you." She smiled, exposing the stumps of her teeth, and advanced into the room swishing her gown. "You're in trouble again."

"Leave me alone." How he loathed Johanna's smile: the crooked shards of teeth and the glistening film of saliva covering them. She had pulled her hair back off her domed forehead. A few greasy strands hung against her cheeks. He wanted to hack at them. They swung forwards as she peered round the room, her head jutting on the thin neck.

"Anton." She was so close that he could smell her sweat and the dank smell of cabbages. "I'll tell you a secret." He could see how desperate she was to tell. Her eyes bulged with the effort of containing the words.

"Let me be!" He lurched out of the door and down the stairs, kicking out at the banisters as though they were Johanna's bony shins.

"Father wants to see you!" she called, but he was out in the garden again. Everything was the same under the fern fronds. The bird was so peaceful, he couldn't believe it was not just sleeping with its head close to its chest and the wings folded. He picked it up to examine it again. The feathers were flecked with silver. He fanned one of the wings. The translucent plumes would never carry the bird up again. He lay it down with the wings folded back. He heard the door to the garden being opened so he shoved it back under the ferns with his toe.

"What are you doing?"

She would have liked to torture him or to be tortured herself. Her piggy eyes glittered in the puffed cheeks. She was chewing something, a hunk of bread. He saw the grey dough moving between her lips.

"What is it?" She craned to see, but he pushed her back.

"Nothing, it's nothing. Let's go and eat; it must be dinner time."

"But there is something, a ..." she began, but he dragged her with him along the path.

"Anton's hidden something in the garden and he won't tell me what it is. It must be something evil he's doing, otherwise he wouldn't try to hide it."

"There are no secrets from God, Johanna. Anton knows that God will know." Barentje smoothed her shining coils of hair and touched the bread and potatoes, as if they were relics…

Anton couldn't get the food down quickly enough, though the gobs of potato stuck in his throat. The mouthfuls were interfering with the idea that was forming in his mind. He was afraid that the thread of reason, once lost, would be gone forever, or that some invisible hand would pull him back just as he was about to discover…

"Eat," his mother insisted. She heaped pickled herrings and shredded cabbage on his plate.

Johanna was chewing with her eyes closed, as if she needed all her senses concentrated on the taste. She ate and ate: a whole plate of sauerkraut, the pink wurst, the oozing ox-cheek. While Anton sat, dry as a stick.

He went back to the garden after their meal. He stared at the body, now stiff and cold. He had killed the bird for nothing, hadn't he? No, it was because he needed to know how it worked and he would have to look inside it, if he was ever going to understand. He knew stuffed birds from his father's natural history collection but here was a real one.

His hand quivered as he held the knife and he wondered what would happen if there was an evil spirit inside the bird. Starlings looked at you as if they had something of the devil in them. They were in the painting he'd seen, herding the human souls into the mouth of Hell with a pronged spear.

He fretted that he would open it up and discover nothing but a chaos of liquid gore. He hoped for symmetry. The organisation of the world depended on the smallest of things; he didn't know, but sensed, this.

He grasped the knife, an old kitchen knife that he'd honed with a whetstone.

Under the skin were the threads of silver like a net worked by a careful hand. He imagined his mother's needle flashing though the stuff she embroidered. He gasped to see the rosy flesh; the fibres of muscles parted by the knife, falling apart, the welling crimson from a blood vessel, its tiny mouth working; then the deeper forms, the petals or roundels, the ivory sticks of ribs; the surprising metallic green of the gizzard and everything perfectly symmetrical, no random chaos of rancid fluids but a secret world of concentrated light and colour.

He opened the body cavity and slit the creature's throat from the breast to the tip of the beak, peeling back the skin from the pale arches of muscle. The eyes glistened in the sockets: deep mauve and indigo.

He stepped back to ease his aching shoulders and saw Johanna's face peering from behind the curling spikes of a plant. She pushed forward and gazed at what he had done, dropped to her knees on the soil.

"What is it?" she asked, because her eyes couldn't make sense of it.

"A starling," he said and blushed.

"What?" she gaped stupidly, "a bird?" She would have liked to understand what was engrossing about it. The light was intensifying the colours. They stood silently before the tiny corpse and she put out her finger delicately, but Anton lashed out.

"Leave it alone! You don't understand."

"I do," she whined. "Let me touch!" The jellied surface of the eyeballs had a lovely sheen. She could almost have licked it up. Her belly was grinding on a void.

He grabbed her arm and twisted it and she, with her nails, scratched a long satisfying gouge in his cheek. They grappled and Johanna, the stronger, pushed him down among the prickling weeds, putting her hot mouth against his ear, she whispered: "He says you're the Devil's spawn and he's going to send you away." She lay on top of him and smeared spittle on his cheeks. Then, she hoisted herself on her heavy legs and scampered off to the kitchen to stuff herself with pudding or at any rate to try and fill the void she had experienced.

Since he was sure she would go straight to her mother, he picked up the carcass just as it was and folded it up in his jacket and took it to his room where he had the space to lay it out and work more on it. He whispered his prayers as he worked, to distract himself from his sister's insinuating words: "You're the Devil's spawn." He said the Lord's Prayer as he slid the tiny bones from their sockets and the sun splattered on the pools of clotting russet.

The wings of flesh he peeled back to reveal the insides reminded him of the angular frames of a rood screen and it seemed that he peeled the layers to reveal a painting, a Byzantine miniature, perhaps.

He drew it, the crayon scribbling like a frantic insect over the precious scraps of vellum, to try and preserve the image that was fading, because if he failed to keep the image he would lose something of ineffable value. Finally he had it, recorded as accurately as he could make it.

He stood back to admire his work but already he felt the urgency of his discovery fading. Almost before he was aware of it he found his hands sliding down, pulling at the strings of his breeches. The image of symmetry he had glimpsed began to form again in his mind as a different ecstasy took possession of him.

The pearly fluid spilled from his erection onto the velvet bed coverings. Anton still had his breeches round his knees but couldn't keep himself from kneeling to examine the congealing liquid. At that moment the door swung open. His father stood there. The older man opened his mouth to speak, but no words came out. He gazed round and his eyes swivelled from the table to the bed, taking in the remains of the bird, the drawing next to it and the boy kneeling by the bed.

In the first moments of his panic, Anton rushed to try and hide his nakedness but slipped and sprawled headlong across the polished floor. A glass decanter crashed to the floor and smashed as his father's sleeve swept across the table. Anton, on his knees in the corner, found himself in a position to closely examine those shards of glass.

"Have I been too lenient?" His father's black coat loomed behind the boy who did not lift his head from the floorboards but lay still as a bird when the hawk swoops. The base of the decanter, a thick wedge of glass, was by his nose, and through its green translucency he watched a beetle creeping.

"It's unnatural." His father was talking quickly in his light musical tones but Anton was struck by the high pitch of his voice. "And the time has come for you to be taken in hand."

Anton noticed that the beetle, as it emerged from beneath the glass base of the decanter appeared much smaller than it had seemed when seen through the glass. His mind flashed with new possibilities: glass, light, and the intricate workings of tiny bodies. His hand closed on the rough gobbet of glass.

The older man spent his rage: threw the remaining contents of Anton's table out of the window, wrenched the covers from the bed, aimed a substantial boot at Anton's rear end and threatened to dispatch him to a seminary where they would beat the evil out of him.

Anton waited; a small smile curled his lip. The light falling on his sparse blond hair made him seem inhumanly pale, yet failed to illuminate the deep-set eyes with their enormous pupils. His father's voice reached a crescendo:

"You will never defile this house..."

He was going to say more, much more, but the quick glance his son directed at him stopped him in his tracks. As his voice trailed off he saw himself reflected in his son's eyes: his petty blundering insignificance. The chill look of disdain made the father catch his breath. It was the point, he remembered in later years, when he'd first sensed a fear of those dark eyes and sought ways to avoid his son or place him at a convenient distance.

As for Anton, he felt the rough edges of that lump

of glass in the palm of his hand; it was important not
to lose it.

Lady with an Ermine

Darkness, suddenly a flash of light, revealing a chamber. The blood vessels spin round—again a flash of brilliant light. Is God there somewhere, or something worse, some dreadful shadow lurking in the depths of the unknown, beyond the reach of the light?

"Nothing obvious." He snaps off the torch. I blink and the surgery returns: books, the leaves of a prayer plant, a photograph of two blond children in red pullovers.

"You've been working too hard, have you?" Dr Vincent balances the torch on his knee. "Zigzag patterns in the periphery of your vision, you say. These are all quite common phenomena." He's very courteous as he shows me to the door of the consulting room. "Do come back if there's a recurrence. But try and rest; try to keep things in perspective."

The bus drops me at the entrance to the complex of buildings. I squeeze past the lowered vehicle security barrier, amble along a muddy path to the rear of a portakabin and let myself in through a shabby door. A smell of damp plaster-board and old shoes hangs in the air. There is the usual faint hum from the bank of computers along one wall. Fluorescent yellow hard hats hang in a row above a line of grubby boiler suits like a comic line-up of invisible workmen.

I open the fridge and take out a carton of milk, take a sniff and pour it down the sink with a sigh. I flick the switch of the kettle and listen to the hiss. All the mugs have a brown scum inside; I select the cleanest. People imagine our research takes place in a rarefied atmosphere of glass and steel: the soft trickle of a fountain in the background accompanied by the rustle of bank notes, freshly ironed by an army of android technicians. I clear a space among the cardboard boxes and old wiring circuits. The desk top is tea-stained and gritty with biscuit crumbs (Swiss creams?) that someone has been eating.

Arriving on the scene before anyone else gives me a sense of satisfaction. I do some of my best thinking at this time of day, before the others start to arrive, bringing their own trails of consequence, their own collisions. Arriving early gives me time to adjust my buffering zones, to establish my points of impact with the thousand tiny shocks I know the day will bring.

It is our job to check the raw data: to sift the results and decide if they will be of interest to future analysts; to look inwards at the precise nature of the matter.

Last night I dreamt of going back to the museum. The building itself was unchanged but I was aware that behind the building, the countryside had been swept away by a motorway. The woods and fields, where I'd walked as a boy, were gone in this dream, and this knowledge oppressed me.

I could smell the honeysuckle perfume my mother used to wear; I catch it now, a faint scent that lingers on the edge of my awareness. She turns to look at me over her shoulder. And suddenly I am back in the dream running to keep up. With my small sweating hand held tightly in my father's, I stumble up the steps of the museum.

Is this a dream, or is it true and happening to me now? I find it more and more difficult to tell the difference. Dr Vincent tells me that this is not unusual – that many people find it hard to make the distinction.

The museum attendant was one of those shrivelled men, so tiny that the cashier's stool had been specially designed to place him at the right height to receive money and dispense little violet-coloured tickets. I never once saw him off that stool. I doubted whether he ever left it, except for mealtimes and to go for a wash-and-brush-up, for he was always impeccably presented.

It was my father who first took me to the museum, after the death of my mother. I think the museum was my father's attempt to help me begin to forget, or at least to lessen the pain of loss.

Thus, it was through a mist of tears that I beheld the shell of a stuffed leatherback turtle, sticky with varnish.

"Once the seas were full of turtles," said my father, poking at a leathery flipper with the tip of his cane.

"Please not to touch!" snapped the attendant in his high-pitched voice.

"...before the delicacy of their flesh made them a prized dish. Turtle soup was so delicious that Ibn Hussein ate nothing else."

"Did you ever taste it?" I asked.

"No."

We moved on to a mummified corpse from China: perfectly preserved teeth in a slack-lipped smile.

"In the Tang Dynasty it was an honour to be mummified, to be embalmed for posterity, so that we can look at him today, and contemplate our own mortality. The fact that we are here at this moment, with all our faculties and in a state of good health, is not something we should ever take for granted."

The empty eye-sockets gazed at us. The head, tilted to one side, seemed to enquire of us what it was like outside the prison of this building.

Any other father would perhaps have thought twice before bringing his grieving son to such an exhibition of curiosities. My father had the insight to understand the rational basis of my grief—that my mother's loss was simply a vacuum that had to be filled. And he was going to fill it: with knowledge, with facts, with the cold hard particles of matter. He knew that it was the best way to help me to understand the brevity of life, the unfathomable mysteries of the Universe and the constantly changing nature of the present.

We paused before a two-headed lizard. The heads were blunt, in seeming imitation of the tail, which was equally blunt, or perhaps it was the tail that imitated the heads. One of the heads peered at us, fixing us with the black bead of an eye, while the other head tore at the bloodied carcass of a chicken that had been thrown into its cage. It held it down with one claw and tore away strips of meat with its tiny, sharp teeth. The watching head was motionless, only occasionally betraying its living nature with a tiny mechanical shudder.

"The dinosaurs," murmured my father, "gazed in just the same way at the volcanoes erupting on the still-warm crust of the earth." He looked down at me but I could see it was not me he was seeing – he was looking beyond me at the spouting lava flow that had opened a great wound in the granite flanks of a mountain. "Who knows what it is that they see, these cold-blooded beasts. Perhaps they're waiting for the ice-caps to melt and for their time to come, once more."

*

I have always kept women at a distance. I watch them drift past, like spectres. Occasionally one approaches too closely but it takes only the slightest touch and they withdraw, hurrying away to warm their frosted fingers.

Only once, a young researcher—dark, Scottish with gold rimmed spectacles... We had begun to sit together at lunch. I think we appreciated each other's long silences. I suppose I might have brushed against her in the corridor a few times. We went on a few excursions to an art cinema and I recall an episode of indistinct fumbling on a sofa bed.

One day, on our way to a seminar, we entered the lift together. As the doors closed with a soft hiss, she murmured something which I only half heard but from which I plucked the word, "love".

"What do you mean by that?" I said. "I like to be clear about these things."

"Feelings," she began to stammer.

"Lust you mean? You feel lust for me?" I was cruel. I felt it rise up in me: the desire to be cruel.

We did not continue to lunch together.

*

The next exhibit was visible only through an eye-piece in a panel of black-painted board. At first there was only an amber coloured glow with something fine and whiskery that fussed at the edges of my vision. Then the long thin lariat of an antenna whipped into view and a burnished carapace, as wide as a car bonnet. The label declared it to be a giant Asian whistling cockroach and indeed, if you placed your ear to a tiny zinc grill, you could make out a faint musical hissing—something like a rendition of a baroque concerto played upon a miniature glass harmonica, but infinitesimally faint.

Something made me recoil from the delicate music: a memory of an afternoon when I had been practising the piano—a little tune my mother had taught me. As he passed the piano, my father had accidentally knocked the lid of the instrument and it had fallen, trapping my fingers.

The attendant became impatient with our slow progress and in his cross staccato he urged us to "move along and give others a chance to view the spectacle" even though there weren't any other spectators beside ourselves.

My father strode away and I caught up with him in front of a copy of "Lady with an Ermine", the original of which, he informed me, is to be found in the National Museum in Cracow. From the time of my first visit, I formed the idea that the woman in the painting was my mother. The impression was so strong that, even though my father had told me that the woman was, in fact, the mistress of the Duke of Milan, I couldn't rid myself of the thought that they were my mother's eyes in the painting, her lips, and her slender hand stroking the animal's fur. I wanted to curl up, like the ermine, on that soft bosom.

I ran home, after that first visit and, on a scrap of paper

torn from a volume of Buchner, I drew what I remembered of that face. My clumsy sketch bore little resemblance, in reality, to the woman's features, but at least I had an image of my mother's face which would soften the memory of the cold waxen mask I'd seen in the casket. He had removed all the photographs of her that were in the house. So that I should not miss her, he said, or form any false ideas about her. He wanted to impress on me the importance of the scientific view. He told me that the artist, Leonardo Da Vinci, was an expert in anatomy and that the hands were particularly well-painted. He went on to explain the structure of the human hand: the network of veins and capillaries and the complex nerves and muscles. If you were to strip the skin off the human hand, he explained, it would be just like the inner workings of an intricate machine, just like those in one of the factories he owned.

When inspecting my desk drawers, as he sometimes did, he came across the sketch I'd made. He picked it up and turned it towards the light.

"You have no talent for drawing," he informed me. "Do not waste any more of your time doing it."

He carefully folded the drawing and meticulously shredded it before letting the pieces fall into the waste-paper bin.

The last case in the museum, a tall deep case lined with black velvet and illuminated by seven small brass spotlights, contained nothing, nothing at all. There was a blank space where the information card should have been. My father always passed it without a second glance, but I often stood for a moment, wondering about the exhibit that had been removed.

We made many visits to the museum. During our visits he imparted to me his profound knowledge of natural history, geology, art and philosophy in whispered lectures under the constant stare of the attendant whose eyes seemed to follow our progress around the exhibition, no matter how crowded or empty the room was.

It was shortly before I was due to leave for America that we came for a final visit. My father, by this stage of his life, was beginning to lean more heavily on his cane and his breathing had become a little laboured as we passed between the exhibits.

The attendant, more diminutive and shrunken than ever, nodded to us and slipped the coins below the desk into his cash tin. I had never ceased to feel the cold criticism of his stare and even as I stood, in a white linen suit specially tailored to my frame, I could feel his eyes following my steps.

The exhibits had changed very little over the years but on this visit we found an impressively large case occupied by a small rusty nail, though so encrusted with orange deposits it had the appearance of a twisted little grub.

"Nail from Noah's Remarkable Ark", read the accompanying text.

My father gave it no more than a cursory glance.

"God is dead," he muttered and shuffled on.

It came as a shock for me to discern the mocking bitterness of his tone. For a moment I began to doubt my father's philosophy and to suspect the signs of a crumbling and distorted faith, like the cracking in the hull of a gigantic ship into which the waters had begun to pour from the gash made by a passing ice-berg.

We had completed the full round of the exhibits and were approaching the exit. The final case which had never, to my knowledge, contained a single thing, not even a nail, was still vacant. My father had already moved past it and stood by the exit waiting for me. I glanced into the velvet-lined interior. What I saw made me smile; I'd caught sight of my own ghostly reflection, dressed in the white suit. I seemed, momentarily, to have been suspended in the case. I adjusted the angle of my hat, pleased and amused by my appearance, then noticed, just behind my head, the pale face of the attendant who was positioned behind me. Our eyes met in the glass.

On the occasion of that final visit, it seemed the time to say something to my father, to somehow acknowledge that we were approaching the end of an era. Soon, very soon I would be leaving home, perhaps forever, and it seemed fitting to say what I'd prepared. Except that when I opened my mouth I found that all the words had become wooden and meaningless.

"Father, I..."

He gave me one of his quick, sharp glances.

"Yes, what is it?"

"You've been a good father. It must have been very difficult."

"What?"

"To bring me up, after mother died."

He didn't speak, merely moved his head slightly.

"If she had lived, she'd have shown me all the things

you've shown me."

"She would never have brought you here."

My father said no more; he merely looked back into the dark entrance to the exhibition hall. I half turned and, out of the corner of my eye, I saw that the attendant, who I'd never before seen away from his desk, had followed us out and was standing, with one hand on the door frame.

When I turned back, my father was already striding away into the dusk.

"What are you looking at?" I rounded on the attendant.

"That's a very fine suit," he spoke in a light, soft voice. "The white looks well on you, young man." It was the first time he'd ever spoken to me.

"Don't call me that. My name is Amadeus, Mr Amadeus." I began to feel hot and uncomfortable in my suit.

"I'm to go to America," I told him. "I have a scholarship to study the physical sciences."

"The earth goes around the sun," he said and smiled. "I know that much. And people may travel great distances in their lives but they always come back to the same place."

The attendant went back to his desk and I was left alone. It was then that I became aware of a muted hum. I assumed that it came from the lighting but it seemed to follow me. Sometimes it was no more than a faint murmur, sometimes it grew to a roar. At times it seemed to disappear, then return almost imperceptibly.

I did not sleep that night, nor would I sleep for many nights. My mind was too full. I'd seen myself, for the second time that day, as I passed the mirror in our wood-panelled hallway. At first I only glimpsed the features I'd always seen. But the longer I stood there, staring at my face, the thinner and more angular it seemed to become and the more my neck shrank into my shoulders. The tailored linen suit was no disguise for the thin torso inside.

*

Here I sit, monitoring the invisible collisions which occur, remotely, at the bottom of a concrete shaft. Their traces, the only empirical data we have for the operation of invisible processes, are measured in a concentric layering of gas-filled chambers.

I mentioned the tinnitus to Dr Vincent; he prodded my ears with a polished metal implement and agreed that it could be. If it gets too bad, I am to go back and see him. But the more I listen to it, the more I am convinced that it is something external – an electrical hum, quite explicable, anyone would say, given my proximity to so much equipment. Dr Vincent maintains that the museum never existed. He says it is the manifestation of an early trauma. He says the lizard represents my sublimated sexuality. Utter nonsense, I told him, but he insisted on the significance of the two heads – the one head denying the erotic impulses of the other. I'm thinking of transferring to Dr Prakash. He may be bald but he only voices his opinions when asked.

I think of my father's semen, the collisions in my mother's womb and his proprietorial paw resting on her bosom. I am my father's son. He has instilled in me the compulsion to analyse the data I see before me. I consider it, suck my pen top and scribble down a few lines of a programme to correct a small technical glitch. Distantly, but distinctly, I hear the strains of a glass harmonica. My mother is combing her hair after her bath. It falls down into her lap like a lithe animal and coils there.

The City in Flames

Jan Knyp opened the pomegranate, as he had opened other bodies; prised apart the rind that parted like old leather and with the point of a knife pierced the tissue that enclosed the red granular cell. The juice broke out over the surface of the table and the lace cloth was stained with a faint orange blur tinged with red as though it had been burned. The fruit had an acrid taste and the flesh of each tiny cell was a glob that slithered in his mouth.

A seed stuck in his teeth so he picked it out with the knife. One morsel was enough. He could not bear to eat— he could not bear to be a part of the world. He felt the clammy sweat that chilled in his armpits and was disgusted by eating, by sweating, by the daily grind, and longed to be free.

It was very dark—as the solstice approached. Who would choose to live through the winter of 1535? Who would endure the weeks of grim rain? The cold that insinuated itself into the clothing, stripping men down to naked and quivering creatures hungry for warmth. In winter they suffered a closeness they would never submit to in summer. Jan and his wife, Regula, were jealous of warmth. They fought like dogs over scraps of heat.

They ate together: a necessary household economy. Yet, the way she sucked up the oysters from their shells; the shape of her lips had something distinctly of the oyster about them: the pink fading to grey, the slackness, the glint of a tooth which could be a pearl hidden in the black mouth—the sucking and dabbing, the half closed eyes; an ecstasy of gorging on the slippery flesh. When she slipped those oysters' lips into her own Jan thought of the consummation of snails, of the smacking of flesh on flesh.

She'd given him one of her looks—her eyes alone were the lean part of her: the pared-down eyelid blinking on the inscrutable blackness of a pupil. "If you've finished eating," she paused with a morsel of food on her fork, "perhaps you can find the time to look over some of the objects we need to dispose of. The furniture we no longer use must be sold."

"There are things I must finish before it gets dark."

"You think more of those papers of yours than you do of this house. You leave me to attend to everything. No matter, I'll deal with the things as I see fit."

He needed to keep his manuscripts hidden or they were employed to light the kitchen fire. He had found his sketches and engraving proofs of the butterfly's tongue bundled into a wad and stuffed into a rotten window frame to keep out the draught. Regula referred to his work as a perversion. She called him a subversive Satanist and told visitors that he cut up animals as a sacrifice to the Dark Lord. She claimed that his fevers were a punishment from God.

His bread crumbled, a gritty substance, quite unfleshlike. He chewed on a rind of cheese. But the process choked him. By the time Regula had moved on to her bleeding joints of meat, he was escaping back to the soot of candles, back to the attic he'd adopted as his own.

*

"Your brother has written." Regula came to Jan's room with the letter clutched to her bodice. "He has sent us a bag of coin with his servant." She held up the little bag and it jingled faintly. "He knows how much we need the money. If you felt any affection for your family you'd write back to him, but I know you would rather sit here inventing your rituals."

"Leave me be!"

"To do the Devil's work. Aye, to eat and drink and do nothing of any use to this rotten hulk of a house. Never, I'll never stand for the Devil's work." Her expression as she delivered this speech should have made him laugh—the solemnity and the peevish set to the mouth. She stepped forward, thrusting the letter into his face. Although the strange symbols were meaningless to her, she was afraid of the writing, of the power of it. She left it unfurling on his desk and stalked out of the room.

7th October 1535

My dear Jan

I imagine that you are in need of funds. I'm sending you a bag of coin with Mathias, he's a blockhead but honest. It's not a great deal, Jan, but it's all the ready cash we have. It's become almost impossible to reach you in Münster. Do you realise that you're all but cut off? Clara begs me urge you to leave while you have the chance. I told her that things are bound to improve and that the roads are infested with thieves these days. My impression is that you might suffer more in leaving

Münster than you would do by staying put for the time being. There are rumours that the Bishop's army will lay siege to the city but I don't believe it will come to that.

I trust that you are keeping well and continuing with your work. Give Regula my best and, God willing, we will meet again soon.

Your brother, Balthasar

*

Before suppertime on the same day, the kitchen boy came running with the news that the city council had been overrun by the Anabaptists. He had witnessed the crowds and the burning of books on street corners.

In the dining room, listening to the resentful clink of cutlery on china, Jan watched Regula as she ate, unable to eat himself. The maid, Gesina, brought in the dishes under their silver covers one after another but it seemed that nothing could satisfy his wife's appetite.

"They've made bonfires of all the books in the city except for bibles!" Regula wiped her mouth with her lace cuff and stifled a belch. "What do you think to that?"

"Not quite all the books," Jan said as he reached for a piece of bread. "I have my library."

"You and your books!" Regula snorted. "As if anyone cared!"

"It may soon be more than books they'll be burning," he said. "Perhaps they'll feel inclined to take revenge for the persecution of their religion and see fit to put to the stake a few Protestant souls."

"You're trying to frighten me, I know." She mumbled the words, as she continued to stuff the pale slices of veal into her mouth. "But still it's a pity you didn't dispose of those books while you had the chance. They might have paid for some of the repairs we need to make."

"I dare say." He watched the maid's busy hands and inhaled her smell of apple peelings.

Gesina brushed together a handful of crumbs and took away the soup tureen. Her strong round arms moved carefully about the table: placing dishes, arranging a piece of fruit. She smiled faintly at the dishes and cups and the tableware gleamed back at her. She herself had the solidity of a crafted object, the swelling contours of an earthenware jug. Her big soft cheeks gleamed with satisfaction in the placid moon of her face.

It was her usefulness that he admired. If only he could have done something useful himself. There were times when he regretted his inability to engage with the business of life. At such times he sensed the beating of a pulse, a concealed core of meaning to life which he had failed to grasp and wondered vaguely whether there might be a sacrifice or a gesture he could make to atone for his past failures.

*

12th November 1535

Dear Balthasar

Thank you for your gift of money. We fare quite well, though Regula complains at the poor quality of the food we can get. "More rind than cheese" she says. I daresay when she is hungry she'll eat it. The city has been declared "The True Kingdom of God"—all property is henceforth to be held in common and I've heard that some are sharing their wives as well as their bacon. I begin to wonder whether we are indeed isolated now that the roads are all closed.

Your brother, Jan

*

Jan moaned in his sleep and twisted from side to side in his sweated sheets. He dreamed he was picking his way across a landscape charred by fire—a fire that flared up in the distance, intensely red against the sky. He'd thought he knew where he was going but he was afraid he had lost his way. It grew hotter and hotter, a blast of foul heat issued from the mouth of a cave. A human figure white as bone, with the head of a whiskered bird, lurched towards him and opened its beak. The eyes like molten glass reflected the flames of the still burning city.

"Where are you going?" said the man-bird.

Jan knew that if he could not tell the creature his destination, then the man-bird would tear out his heart. But, though the name was on the tip of his tongue, he couldn't speak it. Then his mind became blank. He could only stare at the tattered edges of the cave as they flapped in the foetid breeze. It was a soft-mouthed cave, lined with the smooth edges of decay. The hole was well reamed; it had sucked down many souls.

A hot wind whistled out of it with the cloying sweetness of carrion. Jan teetered on the brink of the blackness, on the glistening rim of this maw, his feet skidding on the slimy lip. Some part of him smiled at his dilemma. There was an intoxicating warmth inside, so easy to slip into, and end the prickling doubts.

A woman picked her way towards him through the burning debris. She beckoned him with a bony finger. She had the face of one of the women he had seen labouring in the potato fields, as black and wrinkled as a pickled truffle. Her eyes, large and aqueous, were shot with threads of crimson; the pupils reflected a night without stars.

"I'm dead," she said. "We're all dead."

"Not I," pleaded Jan.

"Not dead, eh?" She began to laugh, a lurching creaking laugh.

"What has happened to the city?"

"Burning," she said, "all burning to ashes."

The thud of the nightmare or the throb of blood was in his ears—the voices still rang in his head—yet slowly the fear ebbed and the grey morning became real. The cold nipped at the lobes of his ears. A smell of burning was in Jan's nostrils, but it was only the maid raking out the ashes of the fire in his dressing room. He watched through half-opened eyes: the way she had rolled up the sleeves of her dress, the haze of golden hairs escaping from her cap. She turned and her cheeks caught a glimmer of rosy light from the rising sun. He watched her haunches swinging from side to side as she polished the tiles.

He put one foot out of bed, his leg tensing with the chill. Slowly he straightened up and edged towards the kneeling figure busy with the dustpan.

"Ah, Gesina!" he croaked, his voice clogged with phlegm.

The shovel clattered on the hearth as the maid stumbled to her feet. "I should've closed the door."

"It doesn't matter; I wanted to ask you something."

"Ask, me?"

"Yes, I have a commission, something I'd like you to do for me; a very important thing…"

"Important?" Her big hands hung down, the swollen knuckles like the tuberous roots of a plant, and her lips worked silently.

"My manuscripts must be taken to Amsterdam and delivered to my brother. I'll make sure that Balthasar pays you for your trouble. What do you think?"

"I don't know."

"It's my life's work, you understand?" There was silence, except for the buzzing of a fly on the window ledge. "I think, after all we've done for you, Gesina, that a little gratitude…" Jan captured the fly between thumb and forefinger and it struggled there, a tiny brittle thing. "I've only to tell Regula about that boyfriend of yours…" he said glancing at her belly. He released the insect and it flew to the top of the window and buzzed there in a trivial rage.

Gesina nodded. He could see she was anxious to get back to her scrubbing and polishing. The door closed silently behind her and he sat down on his bed to pull on a pair of breeches and begin the ordeal of the day that was dawning in a blaze of red.

Jan brushed his hair and examined the yellowed whites of his eyes. He was shocked by the haggard look of his cheeks and the deeply gouged lines around his eyes. He could have been looking at a portrait of his father instead of staring into the steely depths of a mirror.

*

1st December 1535

My dear Jan

Are you sure that there is now no possibility of leaving Münster? A family arrived only the other week, smuggled out somehow. I have a contact who may be able to help. His name is Matthias Bamberg. He may be able to get a safe passage—for one at least. Regula, perhaps, should come here for safety. There is no need for her to suffer.

Your brother Balthasar

*

On the morning that the last of the flour was used up, Gesina, who'd been out on an errand, returned to say that there was a dead man outside in the street. Jan found the body of a man, a Professor from the Anatomical Institute, slumped in a corner where he'd crawled. The russet and brown of clotted blood was caked on his shirt and breeches. There was a deep wound on his neck that gaped like a second toothless mouth. Jan did not peer too closely at the face or look too deeply into the clouded eyes in case the expression returned to him in a nightmare. The man's lips were flecked with spots of blood where he had breathed and coughed his last. He still had a full purse at his belt.

*

"Boiled onions! That's all Gesina says is for sale. I have a mind to go myself to the market and see whether or not she's lying." Regula banged down her knife and glared at her husband. "No-one pays any attention to what I say."

"Oh, I was listening, my little dumpling. I was just calculating the cost of the repairs to the doors when the rabble breaks them down. Do you not know that the Bishop's army has encircled the city and shut off supplies of food? They mean to starve out the Anabaptists and the rest of us will suffer along with them."

"Don't talk to me of those people! If it were not for the house, I would pack up tomorrow." Regula snapped a greasy thumb and forefinger at her husband.

Jan bit down carefully on a dry crust of bread. "It may be a little late for that," he added, glancing round at Gesina who had entered silently.

"What does she want?" said Regula, "I should not be sorry to see the back of her. She is always lurking in corners."

"What is it then, Gesina?"

"There's a man wanting food and the cook wants to know what she should give him."

"Tell her we've little enough for our own needs," said Regula extracting a sliver of onion from between her teeth, "and there is nothing for beggars."

"But he … he demands … Because everything, he says, is now common property and it's his right."

"Demands? Common property? What does she mean?" Regula appealed to her husband.

"The Council of Twelve has decreed that all private

property is now illegal."

"Then we must leave."

"It's too late for that, as I said."

"But surely … we're wealthy. There's always a way for those with money—you've only to write to Balthasar."

"He can't help us now." Jan should have sketched the expression on his wife's face—it would have cheered him in his darker moments.

*

15th December 1535

Dear Balthasar

I was called to a meeting with the Apostles. What do you think? They profess a desire for knowledge. Those who ordered the burning of all the books now call for a demonstration of my skill as an anatomist. I should have refused but there is no way to turn down such men…

They reminded Jan of a huddle of crows: the way they hunched, sharp-eyed in their black rags. Three of the twelve were sitting at dinner. A charred creature lay smashed open on a platter of beaten silver. They scooped out the soft insides.

"Welcome, Doctor Knyp. You find us at our meal. Do you know why we have asked you to come here?"

"I expect it's to do with my religious ideas." Jan looked at the faces. They appeared so ordinary and spoke so softly, but the way they jabbed with knives, skewering the gobbets of silvery flesh…

"You don't believe in our mission? You don't believe in our war against the godless?"

Jan shuffled his feet and looked down at the floor which was littered with charred fragments of paper and the broken spines of books. "Münster is a religious city. The people believe…"

"It shall be swept aside, this false religion. Picture the scene, Doctor Knyp: a harlot riding on a beast, a beast with seven heads. She has tempted the Bishop himself with her beauty; this is false religion. But the day will come when the harlot will be brought down by the very beast she straddles. The beast with seven heads will devour her fleshy parts and will burn her with fire." Three pairs of black eyes gazed at Jan as if he were the harlot.

"Take our beliefs as your own and everything shall be given to you. You shall enter the True Kingdom and be freed from your false love." The Apostle took out a square of linen and began to wipe his mouth. "But you must do one other thing for us. We require you to perform a dissection as a proof that God breathed life into man's soul. We must show people the crystalline heart of man. For it's a thing of great beauty, the human heart, is it not? In that way they'll see that we have knowledge as well as truth on our side. Your findings shall be the basis of our proof. The proof that God created man in his image."

Jan watched the flickering shadows of flames. They reminded him of the innocent bonfires of his youth. But now there was an urgency to the spitting and crackling of the fires.

"And the subject for dissection? It will be a fresh corpse?"

"Oh, as fresh as may be." The eldest of them lurched to his feet. Jan caught the whiff of unwashed body—too much sitting over bonfires, lobbing in books. Winkeldorp, the one they called the Inquisitor, bowed to Jan, "Herr Doctor," he breathed, "do this for us and we'll do what we can to preserve you from the mob. If they knew of you being here in Münster they'd tear you to shreds."

"And your wife, your charming wife, Regula, is it?" said another of the Apostles with a smile, "When will we have the pleasure of meeting her? She's a famous beauty by all accounts."

"She's very shy, she never leaves the house."

"Why so pale, Doctor Knyp? We only wish to speak with her."

"You have a maid too, so I hear?"

"Ah."

A sound of breaking glass interrupted them and the Apostles turned as one, their eyes swivelling, reflecting the crimson light from the window. There was a sound of running footsteps in the street and a staccato yelping.

"The mob is gathering for a lynching," grumbled Winkeldorp.

"Why not leave them to it," said another.

"Would you have them rampaging about the streets? There will be no respect for any authority, not even for the servants of God."

*

On his return, Jan took refuge in his library. He tried to read his Bible but found he could make no sense of it. He could not control the urge to engross himself in some new object of study. He could not rein in his searching brain. Even when he was supposed to be contemplating the Holy Spirit, he was distracted by the physical world, by his obsession with the study of nature.

In a drop of water he found a creature so fascinating that he broke his spiritual resolve: the larvae of a simple animal—a species of water flea. It seemed a miracle of engineering. The fan-shaped respiratory tubes of the larvae recalled the jewelled cogs of a pocket watch, so regular in their contraction and expansion, that they could mark the intervals of time.

While every tavern in the city was discussing the threat of a siege, Jan Knyp stooped over a drop of pond water, observing, under his lens, a tiny water flea as it spun on its axis through the water. The lurid stories of the soldiers, as they burned and pillaged their way beyond the city's defences, seemed but ghostly reflections of another world.

Then the maid, one morning, as she tidied his table when he was having breakfast, upset the glass containers in which his specimens lived. Their world was destroyed at a stroke.

"It's like everything. Subject to a greater force," he murmured, as he watched Gesina picking up the pieces of glass. "We think we are safe in our little world. Then, with no warning, all meaning is obliterated. What a precarious existence is the life of man. None of us is more secure than the tiny water flea."

The maid looked at him, one quick scared glance as she stepped back, glass crunching under her heels.

"It doesn't really matter," he continued and found

himself laughing. He felt very like a man on a small boat in a wide swift river, spinning in the middle of a furious current, drawing ever nearer to the edge of the invisible cascade. His father would have said he was maudlin—that he was too well protected from the realities of life, that nothing touched him. When the maid returned with a brush and dustpan, he said:

"Did you know I have a calf with two heads in my cabinet of specimens? You may like to see it sometime." Because he would have liked to instruct her—or impress her with his knowledge at least.

But the maid was silent as she swept up the last few fragments of glass.

"I have lived a harmless existence," he said, moving the spoon languidly in his coffee, "but still I am not entirely blameless for what is happening—none of us is. Perhaps I should have become a surgeon as my father wanted. Perhaps I might have been of some use."

"I've cleared up the glass. Can I get you anything?" The girl hovered uncertainly by the door unwilling, he noticed, to come any closer.

"No, Gesina, you can go."

If he'd become a surgeon like his brother, his life might have been better. But the idea of the poor with their hopeless ailments: the malnutrition that turned them toothless at the age of twenty; the rickets, consumption and cholera; their pathetic gratitude for useless treatments and cures, their blind faith in medicine. No, he could not have worked as a common surgeon.

*

"He's gone mad!" the maid told the kitchen servants. "He asked if I'd ever seen a cow with two heads. That's what happens to men who are shut up with books all day. Those drawings he makes, they make your blood run cold some of them."

"I heard of a woman who gave birth to three lizards," said the kitchen-boy, as he absently peeled the skin from an onion.

"Oh shut your trap!" said the cook giving him a cuff that sent him sprawling in the hearth.

*

20th December 1535

Dear Balthasar

We are indebted to you for your gifts and efforts on our behalf. With regard to Herr Bamberg, Regula insists that she will stay with me. She feels it to be her wifely duty and, much as I have tried, I cannot dissuade her from this decision. In her stead I am sending a young girl with Herr Bamberg. She's a girl of good family—she can cook and embroider. Promise me that you'll take care of her education and find her a good husband.

I'm entrusting her with the bulk of my manuscripts and anatomical studies…

*

Jan stood at the window that faced the main square. Red light flickered against the sky. The clouds were illuminated from below by the unsettling glow of burning buildings. He thought he saw knots of people moving in the shadows, haltingly, seeking the shelter of doorways. The Market

Square was deserted except for abandoned tumbrels and the skeletons of trees where crows perched.

He heard a noise in the room behind him. Regula had entered, silently. She shuffled, appearing oblivious to her husband, yet her eyes moved listlessly over the silver, the mother-of-pearl, the pierced tortoiseshell of an ornamental fruit dish, empty save for a patina of dust. Her velvet dress hung slack—a sumptuous memory, stained with the meals she'd consumed. She'd grown thin. The flesh hung loose on her cheeks. He saw how her bodice was rucked up these days.

"We must eat something," she sighed faintly. "You have connections haven't you? You are respected. If you can't get food then who can?"

But Regula did not understand that money was useless. The Apostles of the New Kingdom had withdrawn the coinage. There was only barter and begging.

He thought of Gesina, who would be on her way to Amsterdam and freedom. He'd last seen her bundled up in a shapeless travelling cloak, looking very small beside the tall figure of Herr Bamberg.

"You have the papers safe?" Jan had made her open the box so that he could see the bundles of manuscripts as he'd packed them. He would have taken them out to make sure that they were in order, just for the feel of the smooth vellum and the scent of the ink, but the man, Bamberg, was impatient to be off.

"Why should I go and not you or the mistress?" she'd asked.

"Because that's how it must be."

"They say that all who stay will end up on the blade of a soldier."

"You shouldn't listen to kitchen gossip."

When he went to the room she'd lived in—the tiny garret under the roof—he found that she had stripped the bed and left everything tidy: the one blanket folded in four. She'd left all her possessions as if she knew that she was going to a new life—a knitted shawl, the cap and apron; all neatly arranged, finished with. In the mattress was the faint hollow where she'd lain at night. He almost imagined he saw her ghostly form lying there.

*

28th December 1535

My dear Balthasar

I am to give a final anatomical demonstration in Münster. I am to perform a full dissection of the human cadaver. I have been promised a fine specimen of humanity.

Regula took to her bed a week ago and refuses to get up again. I'm afraid she may not live to see the New Year.

Your brother, Jan

PS I've enclosed some observations on the life of a small organism—a primitive life form, which may interest you. I sketched these creatures and was amazed to see that, when reproduced at a size large enough for me to view comfortably, their world became more and more

like a map, or a key to a universe which I had not
guessed at—a universe within a universe with its own
incessant wars and obliterations.

*

As he prepared for his last anatomy class at the makeshift theatre in the market hall in Münster's main square, Jan Knyp thought of the two-headed calf. The heads were beautiful: they floated in their amber liquid, the tiny hooves pawing at the curving walls of glass. The eyes were a misty blue. If this was the work of the Devil, why were they so alluring?

"God or the Devil? Will you go to one or the other? It's a choice you'll be required to make," Winkeldorp had said. "The Devil wants you to be weak and to indulge those sensations which are pleasurable: gluttony, lust, vanity and slothfulness. Forget about those dark places, says God, look up to the light, rise above the earthly passions, strive for the perfection of the soul. Think of angelic things—of eternal joy!" What did he want, to tear Jan Knyp in two? Father who art in heaven! Because Jan knew he was two beings, inextricably linked. Like the calf with two heads.

As he stood above the cadaver he began to feel an ache in the arm clutching the knife. The knife had a handle like those at the dining table and for a moment he was a child again, skewering gherkins. And his mother's mouth was thin with disapproval: "Don't play with your vegetables, Jan."

He raised the honed knife, slipped it between the ribs of the body, like a blade into a pat of butter, and cut upwards. The knife laid bare the layers of fat and muscle and the fibrous tendons twitched against the blade, and then were sundered.

His audience took a collective inhalation; craning necks creaked in stiff collars as he exposed the viscera. He was close enough to see the arrangement of the arteries around the heart, but what could they see, from where they sat, yards away? A mess of gore? How could that interest them? He knew what it was that drew them: the sight of a medical man done up in his black gown, the alchemist presiding over a strange transformation—the silence and secrecy of death turned into theatre. They gawped, goggle-eyed, like rows of codfish in the guttering candlelight.

In the front row sat the twelve Apostles of the True Kingdom, those for whom the entertainment had been devised. Behind their beards they seemed to smile and their eyes glittered.

He sensed the familiar pounding in his head, the pulse of blood through his temples, as if the veins had grown constricted, and the yen of a question forming itself. Was it the Devil egging him on, to satisfy an urge? Was it the Devil putting the blade in his hand: that tool of desecration and knowledge? He wondered where the knowledge was leading him but he couldn't stop. Even if he willed himself to put down the knife, the audience would not let him go. They'd compel him to delve further into the cadaver, to reveal the workings beneath the greying flesh. The braziers belched their clouds of incense. The air was stifling with the heat of many candles and lamps. A young steward swooned and was carried out.

Finally he straightened up, his arms shining with sweat

and the fluids of the corpse.

"Here, gentlemen," he hefted the lump of flesh, "is the heart I promised you. Look well. See what a small thing it is that animates the body of man… or woman." And he glanced down at the corpse.

"But tell us, Doctor, how the soul of man is breathed into the lungs and how the blood takes up the spirit of God."

"I'll leave it to those who know best to explain these spiritual matters." The heat and light stung Jan's eyes. He blinked away sweat and tears. "My duty is done, I think."

"It is not very pretty, the heart," murmured one of the Apostles.

"In fact," said another, "it's an ugly thing."

"Nevertheless, it's the truth." Jan looked down at the torso, "and truth has a kind of beauty."

There was silence as he replaced the heart in the body cavity, arranged a cloth over the body for the sake of decency and placed the knife back in its canvas bag. He heard a whisper as he passed the rows of seated figures: "It's Jan Knyp, the grave-robber, who'd cut up his own wife for a bag of gold."

*

As he left the Market Hall, Jan looked up at the sky. The clouds had parted revealing a black winter sky pierced by an infinity of stars. He could almost have believed, at that moment, in a superior intelligence, though he could not have said what impelled him to such a belief. Perhaps it was no more than the clear cold light of the stars and the sense of an indefinable void at his own centre.

He felt a desperate thirst as he passed a pump. The handle was not quite seized up but, when he tried to get water, all that came from the spout was a trickle of dust. He looked up at the windows of the houses but they were all blank. He would find no comfort there and if he returned to his own house the mob would find him. Regula was dead and he'd done nothing to rescue her. He would not think of her body. It was after all quite different from all that his wife had been. It was no more than an empty shell.

He heard a hoarse shout behind him and he broke into a stumbling run. His boots were mired in clay and he tripped on the wreckage of the abandoned furniture littering the streets.

"It's the grave-robber, Jan Knyp!" a voice shouted. "We'll string him up and cut open his belly for the crows to feed!" Boots pounded the cobblestones. Jan tripped over a bale of velvet cloth and sprawled headlong in the gutter. He heaved himself to his feet and felt his joints protesting. Then a hand gripped his shoulder and he cried out. He felt his sleeve grasped and a strong arm guided him into an alleyway. He struck his head on a beam jutting out from the wall and blackness sucked him to his knees.

*

He drifted in and out of consciousness. Once or twice he thought that a woman was standing over him but it must have been a dream because when he finally came to, in the morning light, he was alone. He propped himself on one elbow and looked around. Smoke hung over the city and the streets echoed with the sound of falling masonry.

Jan watched a figure moving in the distance and was

just beginning to wonder whether he should try to hide or stay still and hope that he would remain unnoticed, when he realised that the figure was familiar to him: stout and solid with a calm and steady tread as she carefully picked a way through the wreckage. She held a piece of horn with some water in it and offered it to him.

"Gesina," he managed to raise himself on an elbow. "It's really you?"

"Drink." She held the horn as he took several sips and spluttered at the coppery taste. "Come with me," she said as she helped him to stand.

"Why are you not far away? Why did you come back?"

"I never left. The man… that man you sent me with, took all the money you gave me and left me in the street. He said it was not worth his while to rescue servants. But I've got friends in the city. There are people who'll look after me."

"And the manuscripts?"

"The manuscripts? They're safe."

They walked through streets that were unknown to Jan, into a district he'd never visited and finally to a tumbling shack. Although it was wretched, it still had four walls and from within came the unfamiliar sound of a fiddle.

As they entered the room, the fiddle stammered and was silent. Jan and Gesina sat without ceremony in a corner. The room was crowded and the faces seemed to smile in the gloom at his coat, ruff of grubby lace and the angle of his high black hat. He thought perhaps they were thinking of the coins in his pockets then he realised that he had nothing, not a single piece of gold.

A young woman with a perfectly round face and blonde hair cut in rough shanks stuck out her tongue, a long pink, searching tip. Her eyes focussed on the end of it. Slowly she brought her hand up to her mouth and flapped her tongue as if was a fan. The woman next to her put out a hand to stop the action of the fan. But the girl pulled away and carried on flapping her hand. It reminded Jan of the compulsive jerking of a dog's leg: an old experiment to demonstrate the action of tendons with which he'd once delighted crowds of students at the Anatomical Institute.

There was a sudden flurry of interest in the room as a woman entered with a steaming dish of potatoes. Several people moved together, vegetables were snatched in bony knuckles. Jan and Gesina were ignored. Only one, a woman with a red scarf, was aware of them sitting quietly in the corner and brought them two potatoes wrapped in her apron. Again there was silence, broken only by breathing and the slow chewing.

Then the fiddle player was on his feet again sawing away at a jig and people began to dance in a frenzy around a brazier that stood in the centre of the room. Even though she looked pale and drawn, Gesina's feet were tapping and a big man with a yellow cloth wound round his head took her by the arm and led her into the dance. Jan watched as the dancers whirled by.

Suddenly the flames in the brazier flared up, a quick orange glare that made the flames leap to the ceiling. It was only then that Jan wondered what it was they were fuelling it with.

The box of manuscripts lay, half-empty, with its lid torn

off.

"It's poor fuel, this stuff. It burns too quickly and sends out too much smoke," complained the man who was tossing the bundles onto the fire. Jan glimpsed a wing he had sketched: a butterfly's wing, with each vein distinct like the spars of a window, and he remembered the colours. For a moment the wing lived again, touched by the gold and blue and the wisps of violet as the flames took it. He grabbed at it to retrieve it but his hand was lashed by fire.

In a panic, he ran for the jug of water standing on the windowsill. He could douse the flames still, because it was his life curling up and sighing softly in the metal cage of the brazier—the hours and days he had spent in a delirium of discovery among those beautiful creatures. He must, after all, save it.

But the jug was empty.

Jan scrambled after the unburned scraps and began stuffing them in his pockets.

"Is it yours then?"

"Aye, a lifetime's study. All for nothing."

The man stared, bemused, as Jan crawled after the scattered pieces of vellum. There was madness in people these days, he thought.

Still the fiddle played and the dancers reeled, drunk with the heat and light. Gesina had disappeared.

Jan sat despondently on a pile of sacks. He had no idea where he would go or what he would do. Yet, since no one seemed to mind him being there, he continued to sit.

"Hey!" Jan looked down at a snotty-nosed boy of five or six. The boy offered him a potato clutched in his blackened fist.

"Thank you," mumbled Jan and he began to cram the steaming floury mess into his mouth. It scalded his throat but the warmth spread into his stomach. With his tongue, he reached after the lumps of potato that had lodged in his gums where teeth were missing.

"This is the end," he murmured to himself and began to laugh gently as the smoke brought tears to his stinging eyes.

"You've got a big nose," said the boy, as he watched Jan eat, "and big yellow teeth."

"I have."

"It's a good fire." The boy thrust his hands towards the flames.

"Yes."

"But it's getting low."

Jan stuck his hands in his pockets, pulling out the remaining bundles of vellum. Together they flung the remains of Jan's work onto the brazier and watched the flames leap joyously.

The Secret Life of the Panda

As Denis stood in the queue at the bank, he noticed that there was a spot of orange on his cuff which he rubbed at to no effect. Marmalade. There had been no time to clean it off before he left for work. He dampened his finger with spit and rubbed at the stain again. The stickiness transferred itself to his fingers. Stains on his clothes made him feel insecure. He imagined other people in the queue had noticed the stains and tugged his jacket sleeve down to conceal the evidence.

The stickiness of his fingers reminded him of Laura's fingers pressed to his adam's apple where he had placed them, the night before last.

"It could be a tumour," he told her.

"I think it's normal for people to have lumps there."

"My grandfather died of a tumour."

"You and your hypochondria."

When they first met she had shown an interest in his ailments and encouraged him to see the doctor. Later on she started to make a joke of his swellings, calling him 'lump man'.

*

"Where's the colour chart?" She was flipping through the pages of the catalogue. The sunlight coming through the window reflected off the glossy paper and, as the pages turned, ribbons of silvery light flicked across her cheekbones and her smooth forehead.

"I don't know." He tensed up slightly, not looking up

but keeping his eyes glued to the newspaper.

"I wanted to check that shade of white."

"Uh huh?"

"I didn't like the 'barley white', it was too pale. I preferred the 'linen white'. What did you think?"

He disengaged his arm from hers. "I'll go with your choice, whatever."

"I don't know where you've picked that up from."

"What?"

"'Whatever', the way you say it: it's as if you can't be bothered to think. It means: 'I'll let you make the decision because I've got better things on my mind.'"

"Actually…" he shifted his position on the settee, still not looking at her directly but aware of her high forehead, the way her hair was pulled back from her face, emphasising her child-like gaze. He had preferred the fringe she had when they met.

"Yes?" She raised her eyes and glared at him.

"They all looked the same to me." He'd trudged round the DIY store with her last Sunday and had tried to be interested but couldn't help thinking it would have been so much comfier to spend the afternoon with his feet up on the sofa.

"OK. I'll decide then. You go back to sleep. That chart must be around here somewhere." She gave him a kiss, but looked as though she might have been tempted to slap him for refusing to play her game.

It was another habit she had adopted: pursuing subjects earnestly and then dropping them as though the object was to test him out. He felt irritation surging in his chest beneath the layers of t-shirt and pullover and was suddenly short of breath.

"Damn it all." He swept the newspaper onto the carpet.

"What now?"

"I threw it out."

"What?"

"The colour chart, that bit of paper."

"Why? I needed it. We'll have to go back for another one. You know we've got to get that bedroom done. Why would you throw out that chart?"

"Because shades of white all look the same."

*

The Old Corn Exchange where the bank used to be, before the new branch opened, had a vast arched roof with baroque mouldings picked out in gold. Looking up into the sky-blue dome was like gazing up into heaven. It was possible to imagine the bank managers peering down from their offices like minor saints.

The new branch had plaster-board panels and mean fluorescent tubes and carpet tiles. It was like queuing in Argos. The grimy off-white panelling (Laura's colour chart would surely have described it as 'cruddy cream') made Denis think of a hospital. He thought of the grubby hands of customers, clutching their wads of money and jerked his hand off the plastic guide rail—you didn't know who might have been smearing their germs on it.

*

On Friday nights after work it was a habit they had adopted to watch the TV together, to slump on the settee and gorge themselves on meaningless television. They considered it was their due after the stresses of the week.

"Denis?" It was that small voice she used, which he doubted she ever used with the primary school kids. "There's something I want to talk about."

He stopped chewing. They were having microwaved chilli in front of the TV. A man on the screen was explaining the desperate situation of pandas in the wild; reduced to subsisting on ever smaller patches of bamboo; breeding programmes were frustrating everyone, including the pandas.

"Yes? Shall I switch off the telly?"

"Turn the sound down, if you like." She tucked up her knees as Denis floundered for the remote control. "Thank goodness it's nearly the end of term."

"Yes, you need some free time."

"There's stuff we need to get sorted out. Things we need to decide."

"Uh, huh?"

"I missed a period."

"It could be stress. You've been working very hard."

"No, it's more than that. I did a home test."

"So, you think you may be pregnant?" He paused and watched her as she huddled into the opposite corner of the settee. "That's…wonderful, love!" He felt he ought to give her a hug, but something kept him in his seat; a sensation of coldness that ran through the marrow of his leg bones, pricking out into the skin of his inner thighs. The corners of his mouth felt stiff as he tried a smile.

"You don't want me to have it do you?" There were angry tears bursting from the seams of her eyes.

"How can you tell that?"

"Well, I just know what you're going to say."

"Oh yes?" He couldn't help his eyes sliding back to the TV screen for a split second.

In the panda enclosure at Berlin zoo several white-coated humans observed a pair of pandas. One of the pandas had climbed to the topmost branches of a tree and was looking down at its mate with an expression of panda inscrutability. The scene cut to a petri dish in which panda eggs were suspended. A lab worker was poised with a glass pipette.

"I don't know what you expect me to say." He slipped a forkful of rice between his numbed lips.

"I suppose I wanted you to be happy."

"I am happy."

"You're not."

"How can you know what's going on inside my head?" He bit resentfully into a sliver of red pepper. Either it was the chilli making his stomach churn or some indefinable sense of momentum, as though he were being propelled at speed in an unknown trajectory. "Can't we lighten up a bit? What's for pudding?"

"A meringue thing and there's a tin of raspberries. That light enough? It's me who's got to go through with this pregnancy."

"It's just that it seems so sudden. I mean, if I don't get through the next round of promotions we can forget about the extension."

"We could always find excuses."

"And you're up to your ears in work. You wouldn't be

happy at home with a child. You're always saying how much teaching means to you."

"You don't understand, do you?" She switched channels. A man stood, braced in a hurricane.

"Understand what? You're not making sense. Would you be happy stuck at home with a kid?"

On the TV palm trees were blown horizontal with the force of the wind. A low building had lost its roof. A man staggered past leaning into the wind. Pieces of unidentifiable debris flew across the screen.

"Would I be happy? I don't know. It's a risk."

"I'm trying really hard to understand but I need time."

"You need time." Laura delivered the last few words tonelessly. She switched channels again. A panda lay comatose on an operating table swathed with white sheeting. A figure approached, extending a steel implement towards the panda's belly.

"Would you be fulfilled if you did have a baby?"

"Probably not."

"There you are then. Meringue?" Denis stood up, piled the plates together and took them out. "Where are the raspberries?" he called.

She followed him into the kitchenette and slammed about in a cupboard. She banged the tin down on the kitchen surface.

"I'll get rid of it then, shall I?"

He was slotting plates into the dishwasher. "We don't have to decide instantly, do we?"

"I've got an appointment at the clinic on Thursday." She had the edge of the can gripped with the can opener and began to turn the little silver handle. The opener was doing nothing; it was turning but not cutting. She grabbed an opener which she hadn't used in years: the one with the solid handle that just needed brute force. The handle, when she hefted it, felt right—chunky in her hand. She brought it down, several times onto the lid and holes opened up. She worked the can opener round the lid and prised up the flap, jagged round the edges.

"Careful, love. You'll cut yourself."

"Who cares?" She went back into the living room and turned up the volume.

Denis woke in the night, aware of the familiar yellow glow from the street lamps and the headlights of cars sweeping across the ceiling. The curve of Laura's body rose and fell, her hair lay tangled on the pillow and her face in profile looked remote. For a moment, gazing at her, he almost wondered if this was a different person, not the Laura he thought he knew.

*

There were two women in front of Denis in the queue with a man in a wheelchair. The man poked out his long mobile tongue and tested the air like an anteater. When he closed his mouth he looked strikingly like everyone else, with his crew-cut. One of the women, in a black lycra top, stroked his short hair and he twisted his head round. The veins in his neck stretched taught, as though they would twang if you touched them.

"Only four tills open, look," she said to her friend. "We'll be here ages."

Does he know what an age is, that man? thought Denis.

Does he sit in his chair and look at the clouds for hours and think: "I've been waiting ages here in my chair"?

The man stretched his legs and waved his shoeless feet. One arm was extended, the veins blue-white inside the membrane of skin; it gestured, almost touching the backside of another lady in front of them in the queue. He made a little noise, a feral utterance.

"Yes, you've had a lovely day today, haven't you?" said the woman with the black top, stroking his shoulders.

They inched closer to the bank tellers in their glass boxes. Was his finger going to touch her bottom? Denis wondered. Did he know what an absolute age this was taking? Stuck in that chair, endlessly with no opportunity to escape from his contorted body, jerking uncontrollably. But suppose that he did know everything that was happening to him; that he sensed that his life was like an hourglass—translucent, rigid, constrained—with the sand rushing through it.

*

When his grandfather was very old Denis had gone to visit him in the nursing home outside Hinkley. The corridors were painted in shining bleached magnolia and he found himself skating along on opalescent lino. The door to the room where his grandfather sat was thick and solid like something out of a nuclear power station. The TV was on. A noisy cartoon was showing: Tex Avery shooting out Bugs Bunny.

The old man was fast asleep in a chair, legs covered with a knitted quilt. Denis could see his grey flannel trousers in the lozenges of space between the coloured strands of wool.

His grandfather's hair was very white and fluffy, moving gently in the breeze. As the Loony Toons' signature tune came up, he stirred a little, like a small helpless animal. His eyes, when he opened them, were very blue, bluer than the technicolour background to the MGM logo.

Denis had wheeled him out into the hot, dry garden to look at the parched grass and the sticks of shrubs. His grandfather spoke in a voice that faded and came strong in waves like a radio commentary. "You've come to take me home Jack," he said, Jack being his elder brother who had died on a French battlefield in his teens, "I knew there were moves afoot to get me out of here."

*

Behind him in the queue, a woman with her hair all over the place was trying to control two toddlers. A small girl was strapped into a pushchair but this didn't prevent her from pushing her brother who fell forward onto his face and set up a bawl.

"Courtney, leave your brother alone, for Christ's sake."

Eventually the boy stopped crying, sat up and, reaching out, pulled himself up by the nearest support. Denis felt the small fingers clutching at his freshly-pressed flannels.

He ignored the child as best he could until he noticed that he'd left stains on his trousers that looked very much like pulped breakfast cereal.

"Sorry," the mother gave Denis a hopeless smile. "Jason, look what you've done to that man's suit."

Jason did not look in the least apologetic. His outsized head wobbled back on his thin neck and he gazed up at Denis with a grin full of the tiny stumps of teeth. He gurgled inanely and sucked on the white plastic end of his anorak cord, sucking and grinning.

Denis read the leaflets: "Save more", "Get more from your flex-account". He reeled off the slogans. It was like reciting a catechism.

The child coughed. If he's not careful, thought Denis, he'll choke. "Spend and save", "Plan your future", he read.

"Please go to cashier number seven." The recorded voice was oddly compelling. Denis stepped forward, drawn to the flickering orange light.

Suddenly he was aware of a high-pitched retching sound just behind his back.

"He's choking. Oh my god, he's choking!" The woman gasped, pale under her fake suntan.

The people in the queue froze and there was a sudden startled silence.

"Is there a doctor?" someone shouted.

The boy had turned a strange ivory colour with blue patches on his cheeks, like an alien child. He lolled in his mother's arms—a thin trickle of saliva snaking from his mouth.

"Where's Mr Hudson?" asked one of the cashiers. "He's the first-aider, isn't he?"

"He's at lunch," someone else whispered in a tone of desperation.

"Oh God!" a voice behind Denis in the queue breathed, almost inaudibly.

Denis had never before used his first-aid training. He'd studied the manuals with a kind of horrified detachment and had never understood how he had gained his certificate, though the trainer had praised his 'cool-headed approach'. Now, he saw himself, as if from a distance, taking off his jacket and hanging it over the rail.

"Let me," he said, sounding more determined than he felt. As if the child were one of the plastic mannequins in a demonstration, he laid him across his knee. The first tentative pat accomplished nothing: the child hung limp, a dead weight. He tried a firmer slap and again there was silence and stillness. He became vaguely aware of a collective holding of breath around him, that he was the focus of everyone's attention, he and his burden. He raised his hand for a third time; the whack he delivered was too hard, he thought. Then, miraculously, something shot out of the child's mouth, a small glistening white object that pinged off the panelling. The child took an agonised breath and was sick on Denis's shoes.

The woman, her hair falling down over the face of her son, grasped him and shook his small body.

"Stupid kid," she moaned, hugging him so hard that her knuckles whitened. The child indulged in a gruff sounding bellow that echoed through the bank.

Denis was kneeling on all fours looking at the ugly black and grey design on the carpet, diagonal lines stretching off beyond his field of vision. The sense of the child's body— its compact solidity and weightiness—was still present. The sickly sweetness of fruit-flavoured chewing gum and the scent of talcum powder clogged his nostrils. His heart walloped the cage of his ribs and he was aware of the throb of blood. His hand tingled from the slap he had given to the boy's back, that small compactness. According to a

Chinese proverb, the thought swam vaguely into his mind, a man who saves the life of another becomes responsible for his future happiness. He felt a sob growing in his throat and was relieved when he found he could turn it into a dry cough.

"You see what happens when you swallow things? How many times do I have to tell you?" the mother kneaded the child in her arms, pressing his face into her breast. He grizzled, muffled against her coat. Denis stood up and the woman glanced at him—"Thanks." She couldn't look at him directly but clutched the boy.

Denis, with a feeling of invisibility, as though suddenly he was of no importance to this drama, looked down at his hands. They trembled and he stuffed them into his pockets, absently jingling loose change. He resumed his place in the queue. People moved aside to let him pass, stepping back in slight fear of the man who had intervened in the slow torpor of their lives.

"Please go to cashier number seven," the same automated voice delivered.

"How can I help you?" She was young, younger than Laura, with fresh cheeks, too young to be cooped up in this place under the artificial lighting. They grinned at each other foolishly.

"I'd like to pay this cheque in," Denis said, as he handed over the cheque. While she scanned it, he wondered whether she had a boyfriend, whether she was planning a family, dreaming of babies.

The note Laura left him that morning, the reason for the marmalade stain, was unlike any note she had ever left, it was terse; as distant as the cold impression her head had left in the pillow which he woke up to. It tied a small hard knot in his gut.

"My appointment at the clinic is at 4.30. Get your own dinner." The note was scrawled on a post-it which was stuck to the waste-disposal unit.

The automatic doors opened but his way was blocked by a pushchair. As he squeezed past he glanced down into a small face; the eyes, a brittle frosted blue, expressed surprise and, he understood it now, wonderment: the intense wonderment of the very young.

*

When he arrived back after work, Laura was already at home, sitting on the settee in the lounge in the semi-darkness.

"Why don't you switch the light on?"

"I didn't feel like it."

"Isn't there anything on telly?" Denis sat down heavily. "What about the news?"

He flicked on the table lamp and caught sight of the two of them, seated at opposite ends of the settee, reflected in the blank TV screen. Their eyes were not visible, just an impression of the dark sockets, huge and melancholy.

Slowly, as if moving with a great effort of will, Laura turned to look at him: "I went to the clinic," she said, "it was a false alarm."

Denis looked down at the white seat covers, slowly smoothing out the wrinkles in a cushion cover.

"False alarm," he repeated. "Perhaps it's just as well, eh?" He thought he should reach out to Laura, and offer some kind of consolation, but the expanse of upholstery stretched between them; a barrier of impenetrable softness.

Paper Wraps Rock

He went to visit them again. They remained, as usual, quite silent. He tried to imagine what they were thinking, so tight-lipped with their staring eyes, but they were impossible to fathom, as impenetrable as if they were enclosed deep in the permafrost or carved out of polished malachite.

It began with a lesson in mathematics. He had no idea what age he was at the time. Memories slithered away from him, drawn by invisible threads.

*

"It's simple," the master said, as a fly buzzed in the topmost leaded lozenge of the tall gothic window. "Two times four is the same as four plus four."

He bent at the knee and brought his head level with the top of the desk. The irises of his eyes were of such a pale hazel that they looked yellow, like those of a dog. "It's not a difficult sum, is it? It's the same as one times eight. You just have to learn the four times table."

Mistakes were marked with slashes of red on the blue criss-cross of the exercise book. Stephen had written out the sums carefully, neatly copying the mysterious symbols. He wondered what he was expected to do with these figures. His mouth was filled with a ferrous bitterness from the rusty nib of a fountain pen.

It was as he made his way home from school along a path bordered by bracken that he first made their acquaintance. They were shy of each other and fled at the first meeting.

He with a pounding of pumps on the dusty path, they with no more than a whisper of dry fronds, a curving broken shadow disappearing with a shiver of grass blades.

It was only later, when faced with the unbending grid of the maths page, that he was able to consider the effect of their sinuous shapes on the harsh lines of his figures, that he began to appreciate the beauty of their forms. Narrowing his eyes he saw a forest of Japanese trees in a snowy landscape. Two was a swan, four a yacht on a calm sea, three was a hinged circle, six—the whiplash of a spermatozoid tail. But it was 8 that coiled onto the page simulating perfectly their graceful departure.

He was anxious to incorporate that understanding of the symmetry or asymmetry of figures into his mathematical studies and used coloured pencils to good effect. However, the improvements were met with red slashes.

"I can't make it any simpler than that: one times eight, four times two, four plus four. It's all the same thing."

The master had a single rogue hair on his cheek that grew out of a tobacco-brown mole. It twitched as he beat out his words on the desk with an ink-stained ruler.

"You'll just have to stay behind until you've grasped it." He stood by the desk and Stephen caught the acidic tang of tweed trousers. At that moment a pigeon chose to smash itself against the glass, leaving the dusty imprint of its wings on the window pane.

The afternoon was fading to dusk when he reached the bracken path. They were waiting, but this time the encounter crackled with anticipation. For a tense moment they grew aware of his danger and he of theirs. After a furtive flickering investigation they seemed content for him to cautiously watch them from a distance. Later he considered their sullen stares, their faint reek of musk and decided to leave his homework undone, attempting instead to reproduce their watchful stillness in the mirror.

They coiled in on themselves—compact, purposeful, precise. Their focus was as sharp as a pin-prick of light. He wondered what it was that they were poised for, heads slightly raised, occasionally tasting the air with a swift tongue.

He tried to tell Daryl Kittle about them, as they were changing for sport.

"They're really beautiful. It's incredible to watch them."

Daryl was busy picking minute clods of earth off his boot-laces.

"You should come and see."

"See what?"

"The adders on the heath. I know a place."

"They're poisonous, aren't they?" He shrugged off his shirt exposing a pale blue-white chest.

"Maybe, but they don't bite."

"Our dog got bitten by an adder." Daryl sucked in his stomach so that the line of the ribs stood out above his hollowed belly.

Stephen struggled into a pair of shorts that were too small round the waist and the elastic dug into his flesh. He stole a sidelong glance at the other boy.

"What are you looking at, lard face?" Daryl frowned.

"Come and see. I'll show you where they are."

"You're obsessed with those snakes, aren't you?"

"What's 'obsessed'?"

*

Dear Mrs Goldberry

As you may be aware, Stephen has been having some problems at school, particularly in maths. He appears to have no grasp of quite basic concepts which I am afraid may hold him back in academic terms. We feel some remedial assistance may be appropriate and hope we can count on your encouragement in the home setting.

Yours sincerely

J Stork

*

As he sat at his desk, Stephen found that it was impossible to focus on the times tables. He could see no point in the sequence of numbers and no purpose in memorising them. He tried closing his eyes in an effort to visualise the sequence, to fix it in his mind, but the image imprinted on his retina was a monochrome coil that unwound itself with the mechanical fluidity of a well-oiled bicycle chain.

"When I set homework I expect it to be done."

Stephen got a whiff of smoky tweed.

"In a few years time you'll be going to secondary school. You have to know how to do simple sums otherwise you'll be punished—made to stand in the corner all day with your feet in the sand bucket.

"Well," he sighed at the hopelessness of the case, "I've done my best. Perhaps Mrs Bister will be able to sort out your problems."

*

Dear Mrs Goldberry

I am sorry to say that, in addition to his lack of involvement in class activities, Stephen is displaying a marked tendency to become withdrawn. I cannot emphasise too strongly the importance of co-operating and engaging with other children in the school environment. We consider that too much time on his own could lead Stephen into unhealthy practices and wish to have your approval and support in limiting his solitary behaviour. I have written to the school psychologist, Fiona Bister, with a view to carrying out a programme of psychometric testing to see if we can get to the bottom of Stephen's difficulties. Could you also please ensure that Stephen remembers to bring his sports' kit on Wednesday afternoons.

Yours sincerely

J Stork

*

Mrs Bister showed him a series of ink-blots and asked him to describe what he saw. Her softly probing questions seemed to go with the sickly smell of lavender and the fluffy angora of her pastel cardigan. She marked responses to the ink-blots on a grid that reminded him of the maths book. She wrote spidery figures in boxes, and scribbled comments.

"What do you see in this picture?"

"A man with a tall hat."

"Anything else?"

"No, only there's a hole in his face."

"And this one?"

"A horse's head."

He did not try to define the expression of sadness or the tears that were slowly melting the face away. The flesh was pouring off the face, but he didn't think Mrs Bister would be able to do much with this information so he kept his mouth shut.

"What about this one?"

He stared at the image and felt the blood rush to his face. Mrs Bister watched him closely.

*

They sat in a field that perhaps had once been a wood or a heath. The meadow was full of ragwort and poppies and lumpy with chunks of concrete. It was now surrounded by new houses in pale red brick which all had the same identical white porches with frosted glass and little black bell pushes. As well as Daryl Kittle there was his sister, whom Stephen had only seen once before behind the banisters of the Kittle's new hallway.

"This means scissors," said Daryl. "And this is a stone." He punched the dry grass down. "And stone beats scissors because it blunts them. Paper wraps stone and fire burns paper."

In no time Stephen was down to his vest and pants. He had a rancid taste in his mouth like old dock leaves and his heart thumped.

Daryl, who seemed to be in charge of the rules, still had his shirt and trousers on while his sister squirmed in her knickers, trying to avoid the stinging nettles.

"OK, paper wraps stone," said Daryl and took off his tie.

His sister put her pink fists behind her back and squeezed her eyes closed.

"One…two…three… Fire burns paper."

"It's not paper it's scissors," she said and burst into tears.

"You're lying and you have to take off your knickers."

*

"And here?" Mrs Bister was on to the next image.

"A blob."

As he watched, he saw that it was evolving into a thing with clinkered flanks, a long tail and a gaze in which flecks of fire quivered and the pupils contracted to pin-points.

It was a creature that knew nothing of time. Hours and minutes were the same as days and weeks; months the same as years. Children and trees grew; houses tumbled and people became old and died.

Over hundreds of years it had basked in the sun's light. As volcanoes erupted, it lifted its pointed head and maybe shifted a coil. As the earth cracked open, it slithered aside a little and carried on staring blankly at the sky.

*

She showed him pictures: a woman's head with no mouth; a pig without a tail. "Can you draw the mouth, the tail?"

A smiling face had no eyes; another had no nose; a rabbit was missing an ear; a child had no spoon. Kettles poured with no handles, penknives had no rivets. And numbers: "Draw the symbol that matches the number. Now continue the sequence: two, four, six…

"Write the answer in this box, no, no, this box."

He slowly began to trace a seven in the box and looked up for confirmation but Mrs Bister's expression was blank, unreadable.

"Here you need to see the pattern," she said. "Tell me which is different."

The boxes contained smatterings of dots. Were they figures? His sight was becoming blurred and he began to feel a heavy sleepiness weighing his limbs down.

"Now look at this sequence. What number should I put here?"

All he could see was a trail of ant-like forms, curiously mobile hieroglyphs, that trailed across the white page.

"They're small."

She scrutinised the face in front of her. She was not unkind, not especially impatient, but it was a long drive to the next school and it would be nice to be back home early as she was expecting a parcel. She glanced down at her watch.

"Time's up."

She scribbled a score on the form which reflected—she couldn't help the thought as it flashed across her mind— the slightly vacant look in his eyes; the occupants of this house had decamped to another planet.

*

In the boys' lavatories it was cold. The entrance was along a passageway that turned a sharp right angle so that what was beyond could not be seen from the playground. The smell was acidic: a sharp stab of urine and ammonia crystals into the sinuses. Three boys turned towards him as he sidled in. He fought the urge to turn and run; the need to pee was too strong. He faced the blinding white wall of porcelain. It impressed dark blurs on his retina.

"Are you a bender?"

He tried to pee quickly, to get it over with.

"Hey, lard face, I'm talking to you." Daryl Kittle had become very beautiful since the last time they had met. His hair was very black and glossy and his teeth were whiter than the porcelain.

The smell of bleach jabbed his nostrils, sending needles of pain into his eyes.

"Are you circumcised? Because we can arrange it for you, cheap; it'll be a quick job, nice and tidy."

Stephen's eye caught the quick dull gleam of a knife. Three bodies jostled for position behind him. Someone kicked him in the back of the knees. He collapsed forwards, his feet slipping into the trough, palms flat against the slippery wall. With one arm twisted behind his back, he craned round. They made eye contact. Daryl's face was a mask, behind which the eyes swivelled. When he blinked, blood pulsed through the delicate capillaries of his eyelids; expressionless grey eyes, each iris a simulacrum of the broken pattern of dots in a chronometric test.

"Oi!" The caretaker stood there in a brown coat that came down to his knees. "What are you up to?"

"Nothing, mister." Daryl surreptitiously dropped the knife and kicked it into a dark corner.

"Well get lost then, the lot of you."

As he followed the others out, Stephen bent to pick up the knife, slipping it into his pocket as he left the lavatories.

*

As he approached their usual territory, he sensed that something was not right. The snakes weaved a restless path between the fronds of bracken. It took a minute or two to absorb the details of the scene: broken in three places, fixed with thick galvanised nails to a fence post, the corpse dangled, head down, limp like an oily rag. The prismatic brilliance of its belly washed to a pale ash grey.

Footsteps crunched behind him.

"Oh, look what someone's done to one of your precious little friends. Shame isn't it?" Daryl's grin was a sliver of white between tight lips as he strutted towards Stephen, his brown fists solid as rocks, as though he knew the rules to this game too.

"It was you?"

"Nasty, slithering, twisted things if you ask me. They should be exterminated. If I catch any more of the little buggers…"

Stephen's ears roared softly. He moved as slowly as a machine, aware only of the weight in his pocket.

*

Dear Mrs Goldberry

I am, of course, concerned about your son's lack of progress in the classroom. We have tried to help, given his obvious need for remedial assistance and his disturbed mental state, but we feel we are unable to justify his inclusion in normal school activities after his

*unprovoked knife attack on another pupil. I enclose a
detailed assessment of Stephen's psychological condition
as prepared by Fiona Bister which I hope will help you
in exploring the options for your son's future.*

Yours sincerely

J Stork

*

In ten thousand years, he thought, all that will have
happened is that the rocks will have eroded away a little
more. Flints, the grey-white nodules of igneous rock, will
have been pounded by the tides, broken down into the
smallest grains of sand. When the land masses shift, the
fields will be a beach once again, washed by salt water.
Perhaps, a hundred thousand years after that, the earth will
explode and the fragments will be burned up in the molten
core of the sun.

In some part of his mind that he had ceased to pay
significant attention to, a small voice was repeating a
sequence of numbers. It stumbled over them, sometimes
repeating or skipping like a badly-learned catechism. He
felt a deep sense of pity for the small voice, at the same
time as he despised it.

He lay in bed with the light off, listening to the sound
of the TV from downstairs. The low murmur of voices was
soothing. He took the knife and made a small cut on each
wrist, surprised at the warm slick flow of stickiness over the
bedclothes. In the light of the streetlamps he watched the
way the tiny flaps of skin opened and closed as if revealing a

new shiny skin beneath. He pressed deeper with the knife, wondering at the lack of pain, as in a dream. His head throbbed with the pressure of blood and his skin seemed tight, as if he could release himself into a new form, a more fluid existence.

*

When Mrs Goldberry went to her son's room the following morning, she found the bed-clothes tangled around something sinuous and slippery: a greyish discarded knot that she couldn't bring herself to examine too closely. "What has he been doing?" she wondered aloud. Her son Stephen was not in his room nor in any other place they searched.

Boys' Games

Clavel looks up at a line of three stars. Orion's belt? He isn't sure. If only he'd studied the stars when he had the chance.

The hard ferrous bitterness dries his tongue, sucking out the moisture. The metallic edge on his teeth sets them vibrating. The thrust of the metal shaft, if it were to advance by another millimetre, would make him want to retch.

It reminds him of a spoon: a small sharp-edged spoon, once silver-plated but worn down by generations of infants taking medicine. The spoon, containing foul lemon-flavoured liquid was thrust into his mouth: "Swallow!" And with that his mother slapped him between the shoulder blades. The demands of six other children made her brisk, unsympathetic. But he knew he was loved; her hair showered over his face as she tucked him into his blankets, "My Rubén, Rubencito."

"Sweet dreams." She always left a light burning to save him from his nightmares.

*

Down in the river a group of boys were playing in the shade of the trees. The branches dipped into the current, a constant movement of leaves and water. The boys were engaged with something beneath the surface of the water, something by which they were both attracted and repelled. They approached it, peering into the water to see beyond the broken reflections of clouds to the dim silted bottom where something moved. They jumped backwards with a hoarse shout, slapping the water and kicking out, churning the mud, then slowly they returned to the object of their fascination.

Captain Bordón watched as they played, wondering what it was that fascinated them. He would have gone to see but he was afraid, afraid that they'd look at him with blank, hostile eyes. Strange that he should be able to issue orders to his men and command them, but that he should feel so shy with these boys. He wondered whether it was because with the men he had a duty to perform, a reason for communicating. Even so, if the men were relaxing, playing cards or sharing a cigarette, he blushed if they looked at him. No, he couldn't investigate the small occupation of the boys.

He caught the odour of rotting fruit mingling with the fainter pungency of excrement. At the back of the guard hut was the latrine used by all of the men except Bordón, who thrashed his way into a thicket of bamboo whenever he felt the urge. The two aspects of army life he had never been able to adapt to were the latrines and the communal bathing. Some part of him was jealous of the men for their joy in each other's company and acceptance of each other's bodies; Bordón bathed by himself after dark.

He turned his attention to the prisoner who had been shackled in the shade of a mango tree. He had been detained the night before as he tried to cross the checkpoint. Now he lounged in the shade, his long legs stretched before him, brushing away the flies that crawled on his face and clustered at his lips.

Of course, Bordón thought, the man was not a peasant labourer, despite his ragged clothes. He'd been wearing a straw hat, coming apart at the edges, a loose shirt of sisal fibre and a July 26 armband. He had raised a deferential arm against the harsh glare of the jeep's headlamps. They could smell the pigs and goats on his sandals. But it wasn't the man's true smell; it wasn't ingrained in his skin, part of the substance of his sweat. Bordón could sniff out a bourgeois intellectual alright.

The man's hands, with their delicate fingers, could never have wielded a machete in the bush. His size alone, forced into the tight peasant shirt and pants, betrayed his origins.

Bordón ran a finger inside his collar to loosen it and advanced on the prisoner.

*

At the village school they called him Chino because of the narrow ovals of his eyes like the glittering carapaces of beetles, so dark that they seemed opaque. When Rubén and the other boys went to swim in the river after school, he stood on the bank watching or crouched in a tree over the water, looking down. "I'm not allowed to swim," he'd said once and so they teased him: "El Chino can't swim, his mother won't let him."

He affected interest in some small creature he had found crawling on the branch of a tree but out of the corner of his eye he observed Rubén and his friends—hung around in the background, his hair damp in the humid heat, his crumpled shirt buttoned at the neck. It seemed that he was always there, but just as he couldn't swim he couldn't play football, so he was never part of the 'gang'.

They always ate lunch—the packages of food prepared by their mothers—in the schoolyard: rice and beans, chicken livers or fried plantain. Chino always had a plain grey glob of steamed maize dough or 'masa' wrapped in a banana leaf which he tried to hide, unwrapping it stealthily in a corner and cramming it into his mouth so that his eyes bulged as he chewed.

One hot afternoon Chino in his sweat-stained shirt with his doughy smell sat close-by, but not so close that it looked as though he was part of the gang.

"What are you eating, Chino?" Pato asked him suddenly.

"My lunch." Chino was trying to cover up his little package of masa when José, who was pissing against the wall at that moment, swung round and the stream of pee spattered off the wall and hit Chino's lunch.

They roared with laughter at Chino, clutching his package. But Chino sat, serious behind his black, expressionless eyes. Rubén stopped laughing, it didn't seem amusing any more.

"I peed on Chino's lunch!" shrieked José.

"Oh, shut up," Rubén blurted out, then wondered why he should stick up for Chino. After all, he wasn't crying over his lunch. He realised he was a little afraid of him, afraid of his isolation. Chino was very strong, sitting by himself. With slow deliberation Chino unfolded his little leaf package, kneaded the contents for a moment and began to stuff the ball of dough into his mouth.

"Chino's eating his lunch that I peed on!" José shouted. "I peed on it and now he's eating it!"

Chino couldn't really do anything to make them despise him more so, after that, they ignored him and he became almost invisible. Like the animals in the fields, he was just there.

*

"So you were heading for Santa Clara?" sneered Bordón, "To visit your sick mother?"

"We may as well drop the pretence." Clavel spoke with the quiet dignity of his rank. "You can see I'm no peasant labourer. I was going to Santa Clara to join up with reinforcements. There are a thousand members of the National Guard entrenched in Santa Clara. Your intelligence should have let you know."

"We intend to march into Santa Clara before the end of the week."

"It will be impossible to root out the National Guard. They're too powerful, even for the rebel army."

"You'll never hold the city." Bordón swiped at flies with his cap. "And you know why? Because the National Guard has no popular support. The people won't help you."

Clavel was watching an egret hunting along the riverbank. It searched with sharp yellow eyes, peering intently into the reeds, thrusting its long head this way and that.

"You have a reputation, Captain Bordón," said Clavel, his eyes fixed on the egret.

"Is that so?"

"People speak well of you within the National Guard, it may surprise you to know."

Bordón curled his lip and snorted with laughter.

"People say that you are respected," Clavel continued, shading his eyes against the midday sun, "more than any other commander in the rebel movement."

"And which people are they? The bourgeois commanders of the National Guard? Power belongs to the people, that's my belief."

Clavel watched the egret as it probed delicately in a patch of mud. He spoke carefully, knowing that he was taking a risk with his words: "That's what the socialist propagandists tell you. That's how they compel you to work like a dog, carrying out their orders. But your leaders will never recognise that; they want all the power for themselves. They will never reward you as you deserve."

"My reward is in serving the people."

"Is that true?"

"Our orders are to shoot deserters from either side."

"I'm not a deserter."

The egret picked its way slowly through a patch of water lilies that glimmered in the gathering dusk. The feathers were so fine and white, they reminded Clavel of the white shirts he used to wear to school.

*

Chino was sitting by himself watching the oily surface of the river when someone sat down beside him. It was Rubén. If he'd been asked why he did this, Rubén would not have been able to say. It was just that the river and the silent boy sitting there seemed to draw him.

Chino carried on sitting, motionless. He would have reached out to touch the clean white sleeve of Rubén but his damp fingers trembled and pulled back. He knew, however, what the cloth would feel and smell like. He sat, pulling the leaves from the twigs that overhung the water.

"What are you doing?" Rubén slashed the trunk of the

tree with a dead branch.

"Nothing."

"Tell me what you're thinking."

"Chino doesn't think," said Chino and continued systematically stripping the leaves, until his fingers were stained a greeny-brown. His eyes were blank as pebbles. It was true, you could never tell what Chino was thinking.

*

Lieutenant Carvajal appeared in the doorway of the guard hut, balancing a tin plate of food, which he handed to Bordón. Taking the plate, Bordón hesitated then jerked his head towards Clavel. The lieutenant disappeared and returned a moment later with a plate of fried plantains and rice for the prisoner.

Clavel chewed thoughtfully on a strip of plantain. "It would be good to take a dip in the river." A bead of sweat formed on Clavel's upper lip, trickled down his neck and settled in the hollow between his collarbones. "I'll splash some water on my face and chest. It won't take a moment."

Clavel peeled the shirt over his head and went down to the river's edge. Behind him in the dusk he heard the snap of a safety catch; a tiny metallic noise that echoed across the river. For a moment he froze, then slowly he advanced to the water and knelt in the dry leaf mould. The river lapped at his fingers. He remembered his mother calling out to him: "Come on in now, Rubén. Your dinner's ready." He cupped water in his hands letting it trickle through his fingers.

Bordón chewed on a piece of bone, tearing off strips of flesh with his big yellow teeth. He watched Clavel crouching and dabbling his hands in the water. He was thinking of a time when he'd stood watching the other boys bathing.

Clavel scooped up water into his face and allowed handfuls of water to run off the back of his neck down his spine. Mosquitoes gathered on his shoulders where the skin was damp. He didn't seem to mind them. Slowly he stood and turned to face Bordón.

"So," he said, drawing out the words thoughtfully, "the rebels will consolidate their hold in Santa Clara under the command of Captain Bordón."

"You mock me."

"Not at all." Clavel turned up his palms in an attitude of helpless innocence. Holding his shirt in one hand, he tucked the thumb of his other hand into his belt loop. He closed his eyes for a moment. Drops of water fell from the fringe of his dark hair onto his heavy eyelids. He looked as though he could sleep in this standing position. Bordón noticed a streak of mud across the other's chest and felt a sudden compulsion to wipe it away, to restore symmetry.

*

In the soft warm mud at the river's edge Rubén and Chino constructed elaborate edifices, castles in which doors and latticed windows were carved with a stick.

The silver shadows flickered. The sunlight fell on the water and a faint breeze brought the scent of blossom from the orchards. Chino glanced sideways at the downy skin of his friend Rubén. He wanted to speak but his mouth was gummed up; the seams of his dry lips twitched. It was a wordless time as they moulded the mud into the foundations of walls and turrets. Only when Rubén murmured, "That's a good tower." Chino unglued his lips to whisper: "Like the one in Santa Clara." Being with Rubén was like holding something ineffably fragile like an egg and trying not to crush it. He sat with his elbow scarcely touching Rubén's sleeve and his happiness was like a warm full belly.

Rubén made up stories about the people who lived in the buildings and they lost themselves in the world they'd created. Chino's face shone with the light reflecting off the water. He looked up to see José peering at them from the shade of the trees.

*

Rubén had been thinking about Chino a lot, the hungry look of his slightly protuberant eyes. He was thinking about giving him one of his fishhooks. His uncle had given him seven steel hooks. Chino didn't have much. The family was so poor they had no money to repair the oven and that's why Chino's mother couldn't cook the maize dough like everyone else.

Chino would be grateful for one of the hooks. Perhaps it would make up for the way they had treated him. He chose a hook with a tarnished shaft and wrapped it with some scarlet thread to hide the spoiled steel.

After school the next day, the air was full of buzzing insects, tiny plaguing sand flies that pricked them all over.

At first Rubén thought Chino was going to cry. His mouth was turned down at the corners. "It's a fishhook, a good one," he reassured.

"Yes, I can see."

"Is it OK?"

"Yes, a fishhook is always useful."

"My uncle has lots of them."

Chino grabbed Rubén's arm in a clumsy movement and held on to it, twitching as the sandflies pricked.

"I have to go," Rubén tried to pull his arm away.

"Thanks."

"Don't mention it."

Rubén almost wished he hadn't given the hook. Chino stood close up. He was shorter than Rubén and only came half way up his shoulder. He sweated in the still shade, brushing sandflies away from his mouth.

"See you tomorrow." Rubén walked briskly away, certain that Chino was going to follow, dogging his footsteps, but when he looked, Chino was gone.

A week later Chino sidled up to Rubén in the schoolyard and offered a package. At first Rubén thought it was going to be one of the corn dough balls because it was wrapped in a leaf and about the same size. Instead, he found a small gold brooch set with an ugly seed pearl. The kind of thing old ladies wore on Sundays.

"It's yours," said Chino looking out of the corner of his eye.

"I can't take this," Rubén began. "It's too…"

"You have to have it," Chino whispered urgently. "I want you to have it."

"I can't take it. You have to give it back."

"You think I'd give you something I'd stolen?" He got up close so that Rubén could smell dough balls.

"Of course not, Chino."

"You're my very best friend," whispered Chino.

Across the yard, the gang sauntered towards them: Gaucho, José and Pato. Rubén tried to push Chino off in a panic but Chino held on so that finally Rubén had to thrust him off with both arms. The package and its contents fell into the dirt. Rubén kicked it away, terrified that someone would see it: the love token.

When he glanced round, Chino was gone. A week later Rubén found the fishhook wound with red thread, on his desk.

*

There was a fly crawling on Clavel's nose but he could do nothing about it; Bordón had bound his hands behind his back. He sat in the sweltering shade, waiting. He watched a trail of ants transporting pieces of leaf down the trunk of the mango tree. He reflected that the ants shared a common purpose and that he had never had this sense of purpose, that he was lost. The thought came to him that he would die, here in the Sierra at this forsaken checkpoint with a rebel bullet in his head.

He was jolted out of his reverie by the sight of Bordón, emerging from the door of the hut, wild-eyed. "I remember," said Bordón thickly, "when I first came to the Sierra, they couldn't understand me. The way I spoke, they said, was alien to them."

Clavel looked at the sweat gleaming on Bordón's upper lip, his thin hair, but said nothing.

"I've been here a long time. I belong here now."

"Of course," Clavel murmured. He could smell the alcohol on Bordón's breath.

"You're the outsider. It's you who has no place."

Clavel glanced down at the stream of ants still trailing across the path. "Perhaps neither of us belongs in this place. We are neither of us suited to a life of labour. We want too much for ourselves."

"You think that you can say what you like to me. You think that because you're an officer that I have to respect you, hand you over to the authorities for a fair trial. Before our family came to the Sierra, long ago, my mother had a job cleaning. She cleaned the homes of the rich people in the city. She lost her job because she was accused of stealing, but it was a lie because she never stole a thing. My father laboured in the cane fields. He worked so that he could afford to rent a piece of land. Then, we left the coast and came to the Sierra. We thought things would be better. It took a long time for people to accept us. Now you are the outsider and you don't understand our lives. You don't understand what people want. They want a better life. They want justice."

"We all want a better society and a more democratic government."

"Don't come at me with your smart ideas, Clavel."

"I'm just talking about progress."

"Oh, I know your kind of progress. I've been to Havana and seen the corruption for myself at first hand. I've seen the money and the luxury cars and the prostitutes on the waterfront."

"Even they have to live somewhere."

"Well, I'll tell you, Clavel. When the rebels take over, all that will be swept away. There'll be nowhere for people like that in the new society. We shall know how to deal with them. They won't pollute the new country. There'll be no place for them."

"You seem very sure of that." Clavel smiled, a tired, benign smile.

"You're laughing at me, Clavel."

"Not at all, you're mistaken."

"I can tell when I'm being made a fool of."

*

Clavel sat for a long time listening to the sound of Bordón, crashing about drunkenly in the guard hut. He sat quietly, so still that a lizard ran up the leg of his trousers as if the man had become a part of the tree trunk. Poised on his knee, the tiny creature cocked an eye up at Clavel. He observed its pulsating throat; it was as though the creature's heart was in its mouth. He felt his own breathing—a shallow palpitation. It occurred to him that Bordón had lost his mind in his drunken state.

The dusk crept along the fringes of the river, bringing clouds of biting flies, tiny black points of irritation. He heard Bordón issuing a curt order, to no one it seemed: "Pull yourself together man. Stand to attention!" It was as if he were dealing with a particularly raw recruit: "Stand to attention, I said!"

Clavel's mind wandered to his flat that he'd left last Sunday. He imagined the chair by the bed on which he placed his alarm clock and the photograph of his mother. He had left his clothes scattered around because the cleaner would be coming to tidy up. He left money on the kitchen table and, as he left, he had taken one last sniff in the dim hallway. He tried to recall the smell that his flat had.

*

The lieutenant appeared in the yard, his face streaming with sweat: "Those boys are back, Captain. I can't keep chasing them off. They think it's a game. You might come and have a word with them."

"Lieutenant, you are continually interrupting. I'm interrogating Colonel Clavel. Deal with the boys yourself, or are you scared of them?"

"No, sir."

"Then do it. If you interrupt me one more time I'll have you disciplined. I'm serious, Lieutenant Carvajal. One more interruption and I'll have you arrested." Bordón's voice cracked.

The lieutenant exchanged a look with Clavel as he turned to go.

After the youth had shuffled off, Bordón turned to Clavel: "You're trying to undermine my authority with these men."

"No."

"I saw you exchanging smiles with the lieutenant."

Clavel was silent.

"I know when I'm being undermined."

Clavel picked up a leaf and examined it slowly.

"You're trying to corrupt my men, to get them on your side."

"You're in charge here, Captain Bordón; I'm just a prisoner."

*

On his watch, later in the night, Bordón looked in on the

prisoner. He lay face down, his left arm under his chin, his right arm by his side, the palm splayed upwards. His damp hair glistened in the dimness. His shoulders rose and fell rhythmically but the rest of his body was motionless. His eyes flickered open. He turned onto his back, rubbing his eyes.

"What's up, Bordón?" His hands hovered in a strangely animal gesture above his chest. "It's not morning?"

"No, Clavel."

"So?"

"I wanted to ask a question."

"In the middle of the night?"

"Do you... Do you believe, Clavel, in God?"

Clavel's mind was blank. He noticed the moon hanging in the sky above the gurgling river. When he was four or five, Clavel had woken in the night and, seeing the moon shining into the room, had risen to go and stand in its crisp cold light. As he stood there cloaked in white light he had had the sense of being completely alone, despite the sleeping bodies of his brothers all around him. It was as if the moon indicated a pathway to him alone and that, if only he could follow the path to its conclusion, he would discover some truth.

The moon shone now, surrounded by a frosted violet corona. He'd been a sentimental child: the sight of the moon was enough to make him weep for something he couldn't have put into words. But the army had pushed those things deeper, so deep that now he could only shiver slightly at the memory.

"I really don't know what I believe."

"That's no answer."

"It's the only answer I have."

*

"Lieutenant Carvajal?" Clavel croaked through cracked lips, waking in the night.

"Yes?"

"Would you mind fetching me a drink of water?"

"There's a pitcher of water by your bed."

"Yes, but my arms are tied."

"I forgot."

"Could you?"

Carvajal, fumbling in the darkness, collided with Clavel: "Sorry, my night vision isn't good. I've got the water here. What's that?"

"My leg."

They laughed, brushing against each other in the darkness.

"Is that your mouth?"

"Hold it still, I can't…" Clavel gulped quickly between stifled giggles.

*

Bordón stumbled towards sounds from Clavel's hut. With each step, his heart pounded in his chest. The leaves crackled underfoot. The silvery fronds of the cohune palms shivered against the night sky but the path was invisible— it would be easy to step on a snake in the darkness.

Only the other night there'd been a shout from one of the men: "A snake!" He'd surprised the creature as it crossed the road outside the guard hut. The men cudgelled it with a rifle butt—it lay twitching in the rain, writhing, catching the light of the flickering lamp, its small head darting from side to side even though the body had been crushed.

"A harmless thing," Clavel had said, "One of those which catches rats in the roof. You shouldn't have killed it."

Bordón had been furious. "If the men want to kill a bloody snake then I let them. There are enough of the damned things round here."

As he approached Clavel's hut, Bordón heard whispers and sudden spurts of suppressed laughter. They were in there together, Clavel and the lieutenant. The night insects churred complicitly. Bordón listened; he was convinced he heard his own name. Against his thigh he felt the comforting weight of an Argentinean pistol. He ran his hand down the smooth gunmetal. The tiny ridges along the barrel had a comforting precision. He hefted the pistol in his podgy fist.

Finally he stood in the doorway of the hut, letting his eyes adjust to the gloom. Against the far wall was Clavel's bunk and he saw two figures embracing there; two men kissing. Bordón heard the wet gulping. He didn't wait to see more.

Bordón pushed Carvajal aside and dragged Clavel out of the hut, kicking him from behind so that he crumpled forward, unable to break his fall because his hands were tied. Bordón yanked him into a kneeling position and took the pistol, ramming it hard into Clavel's mouth.

He thought of the young man they had executed a month before in the Sierra for passing information to a member of the National Guard: Bordón's first execution. The lad just knelt there, as the gun was pressed to his temple; Bordón had been so focused on the moment that there had been no room for any other idea, any regret. He'd pulled the trigger, tensing his arm against the pistol's kick and hoped that he didn't get too much gore spattered on his uniform because there would be no chance to wash it off. Then, it was done. He felt numb with the finality of it, the noise of the shot ringing in his ears. The body fell slowly, heavily, the muscles giving way. Bordón had tried not to look in the eyes in case he recognised that look of blank indifference which was so terrifying; he'd looked away and allowed others to cart off the corpse and bury it in some hole at the side of the road, in the hope that the boys who always played by the river did not notice the shot and did not come across the evidence later.

*

The stars are sprayed like fiery droplets across the sky. There's a cold ache in Clavel's stomach; he tries to shift his position to relieve the sense of nausea.

"Stay still!" The shaft of the pistol jabs into the back of his throat and Clavel forces himself upright. The whine of insects resonates in the still air. The sound is drawn tight as if at any moment it will snap, exploding into a silvery kaleidoscope of silence.

His heart beats, a hollow thrum that doesn't belong to him, or anyone.

"Goodnight," she'd say, her hair falling softly. The taste of guavas is in his throat, almost blocking out the acrid flavour of the metal.

He takes one breath after another, drawing out the moments. There is a sudden flash, a crashing, a fracturing of the glistening night sky—all the stars rushing towards him, sucking him into their white light.

Cut Short

I am waiting to get my hair cut, leafing casually through the paper while the barber finishes off the man ahead of me, who has a full head of crisp grey hair. They are talking about sport: a remarkable wicket or some such. In the paper my eye is caught by a photograph; a blurred mug shot. The head half-turning towards us, the expression inscrutable. I look for eyes but, apart from a faint darkening and the impression of a hollow, I can see no sign of eyes. The photograph is of a dolphin, the Yangtze River dolphin.

"Would you like any gel on that?" the barber asks his customer.

Apparently scientists have spent several months searching for traces of the dolphin along the Yangtze River. I imagine the surging confluence, wider from shore to shore than the eye can see, and a lonely little boat with three men in it, trawling microphones.

The Chinese came to revere their river dolphins. In ancient times they were thought to be the reincarnations of dead princesses, but more recently the Cultural Revolution abolished the myths just as it swept away all the sacred places or allowed them to fall into decay.

The dolphin in the picture has teeth, a row of tiny juttings in its beak-shaped snout. It seems to smile. Not much like a princess, I think.

The barber is ready for me. He flicks a voluminous black nylon cape over my front as though he's setting the table for a meal—a wake perhaps. I catch sight of myself in the mirror, my thinning hair.

Those dolphins…, I want to say, but don't.

The cricket on the radio has finished. They're interviewing the mother of the kidnapped child. Why, the interviewer asked, did she stay in Portugal? Because, the mother explains, she just felt it was the right thing to do. Perhaps she couldn't bear to resume her life; it would be admitting that the child had gone. Going home to try and pick up the threads of a life unpicked, to try and weave them together again, would be hard.

The scientists who searched for the dolphin along the Yangtze had gradually lost hope, the news article said, of finding any dolphins alive. After visiting all the best locations—the hot spots—they'd reluctantly begun to lose faith in their search.

You could imagine the Chinese peasants clinging to the last traces of their beliefs, secretly visiting the shrines and temples they had visited for generations, retelling the old stories, stories of patience and endurance, of the spirits of people reincarnated in trees and rocks and dolphins.

The barber tugs at my hair. "When was it you last came? Early May?" I couldn't quite remember when it had been, late June I thought. "These tufts have grown fast," he says, pulling at what's left of my hair at the sides.

My brother wrote a blog when he was in Thailand last year, in which he described a visit to a Buddhist shrine in the hills. The tourists make the pilgrimage up the rocky path in the heat along with the Thais. According to my brother, the tourists are rather cavalier in their attitude to the shrine. They complain of the heat as they toil up the path and are surprised when they reach the summit at the lack of facilities or refreshments, as if they'd expected to find a sandwich vendor or a coke machine. Westerners don't really "do" faith, unless it's faith in their possessions or their families.

The woman in Portugal, I've seen photos of her too, handing out leaflets, has a haunted look. She's unable to admit that the search is over. She has to keep faith. She hands out photographs of her daughter to passers-by. I imagine each alleged sighting in a restaurant in Holland or Greece, is like a whisper of faith to her.

"It's better short, isn't it?" The barber is clipping off what's left of my back and sides, he's revealed the full extent of my thinning scalp. "Yes," I agree, "it's better."

I saw my brother at Christmas on a web-cam from Thailand, out of synch with his voice. The image was jerky, uncharacteristic for my brother who is not given to rapid movements. He'd had all his hair shaved off and his scalp shone. He'd looked very much like one of the Buddhist monks pictured on his blog and I wondered whether he'd gone native, but he sounded the same: his northern cadences overlaid with southern vowels.

"Your head's very shiny!" was all I'd managed to say before the web-cam crashed.

The eye of the web-cam brought me an image of my brother 7,000 miles away, about as far away as eastern China. It wasn't a good image; it needed me to fill in all that was lacking from the grainy patchwork of pixels, to make it look like my brother. Somehow it was a disappointment, as though I'd been cheated out of something.

On my father's windowsill there's a picture of my mother. She's half-turning, not looking at the camera. It was one of those pictures that I'd never really looked at when she was alive. It wasn't a particularly sharp image or a good portrait but after she'd died I pored over it just as I'd pored over the photo of the dolphin, seeking for something of her in its blurred lines. Was this all, I found myself wondering, that's left? And, horrified that I might begin to forget, I began to assemble all the photos that I had, scouring my drawers for snapshots, even the bad ones, of my mother. Perhaps it's like that for the mother of the kidnapped child, perhaps distributing the image everywhere is a way of keeping her present, of keeping faith in the possibility of her discovery.

The scientists have reluctantly pronounced the Yangtze river dolphin extinct. All that remain are photos, sound recordings, a few preserved skeletons. It's not enough, but it's all that's left.

The barber holds up the mirror to show me the back of my head.

"How's that?"

"Fine thanks." I can see now how I'm going to look in my old age. After each visit to the barber, I look more like my father. In a few years' time I'll be as bald as he is.

The river dolphin has a similarly bald pate in that photo: emerging from the cloudy waters to peer at the camera lens, grinning with its comb-like teeth, an unlovely princess. I wonder, if they are now gone forever, where the souls of the dead princesses will go.

The Rabbit Keeper

It was a hot summer evening. The swifts were shrieking outside the bedroom windows and at the end of the garden, where the sun was setting, a line of poplar trees pricked the bloodied sky.

Alexander's mother was wearing a dress that had a design of birds in ornamental cages. There was a thick black belt around her waist. She was speaking in her funny voice for visitors and he knew that Carol was coming to baby-sit.

Carol had a black and white rabbit with dark knowing eyes, like a rabbit in a picture book. It had babies nestling in the back of the hutch but you couldn't play with them because the doe would get nervous and eat them. He imagined her, setting about them, biting off their heads.

Her father was a doctor. He had worked overseas and got some disease that had left him yellow and crumpled like a wash-leather left to dry. It was this that made him seem special—enviable even.

Carol had round brown arms that swung heavily from the sleeves of her violent pink dresses. Alexander liked it best when she told him stories of African bees as big as apricots with stings that made their victims swell up like purple balloons and die screaming.

She was going to be downstairs with Vic, and Alexander was not to create trouble.

I don't like that man, he informed his mother.

What's wrong with Vic? He's a perfectly nice young man. And he has to take Carol home afterwards.

She only lives next door.

He listened in furious silence to the story his mother read to him.

...and the wolf gobbled him up. She flicked off the light.

What happened then?

The wolf ate him—that's it.

Is that the end then?

Yes.

Did the wolf take his clothes off before he ate him?

Of course not.

Did he die?

Yes, now off to sleep with you.

Out of a dense, dark thicket the wolf loomed with his hot red mouth and his long wet tongue and glistening teeth. Alexander squirmed, feeling the fangs on his legs. Feet first he went, down into the animal's stomach. The lolling tongue dripped saliva over him as he went.

The wolf's breathing was loud; it seemed to come from his mother's room. Above him the ceiling revolved slowly, a changing pattern of yellow light, as a car passed. The window frame buckled and the curtains billowed like swans flapping their wings in fury. There was a noise like an animal in pain and a man's deep-throated laugh.

Mum, Alexander called. The laughing stopped.

Mum?

Your mother's coming back soon. It was Carol's voice.

There was a very long silence and then more laughter, cautious nervous gulps of suppressed hilarity.

Alexander waited a while then shouted in a louder voice: Mum!

There were sounds of feet, or sinister paws, padding across the landing carpet. Vic's head appeared in the bedroom doorway.

If little boys call for their mothers one more time... Vic peered blindly into the darkness but Alexander could see him, outlined against the door frame with the raffia lampshade swinging behind. He shut his mouth tightly and pulled the covers over his head. The footsteps retreated.

*

It was a hot buzzing day in July. Hover-flies, cabbage whites and bees swarmed in the sunshine.

He lay in the shade of the laburnum tree, picking up the little twisted pods that were scattered across the grass. He lay back with his arms behind his head and peered at the sky through the branches of the tree. It was a cold sky, despite the warmth of the day, a hard shiny blue.

The seeds of laburnum were very poisonous. They looked innocent enough, with their green and black mottled bodies lined up in their pods like tiny bullets. Alexander plucked out one or two and tasted them. There wasn't much to them—a slightly acrid sensation on the tongue. He decided it was best to steep the seeds in hot water to make the poison come out then mix this with orange juice which he would somehow get his victim to drink.

*

Vic was the real culprit. He had made Carol forgetful and full of a kind of soppy sadness. Alexander saw her sitting in her upstairs window or on her swing in the garden and knew that Vic had stolen her away, scooped her out and left her with nothing on the inside except pulp. He was making Carol ill and Alexander had to do something.

He ground the seeds into a paste and mixed it with orange squash. He took it next door with him. Vic was sitting on the swing with Carol on his lap. She was looking pale and unhappy.

I've found a nest of wood lice.

That's nice.

Nice was for lavender bath cubes and gold doilies and caramels. This was proof that Vic had rotted her brains out.

I've brought us some orange squash. He held out the tray with the two cups and one glass.

What a funny kid, said Vic. We'll get you an apron for your birthday so you can be the real lady bountiful.

But Alexander was pleased when Vic raised the glass to his lips.

I'm going into Stockport, Vic announced, to buy that new single by The Rolling Stones. I met them once you know, in a pub.

How did you know it was them? Alexander asked.

Nobody's speaking to you, sneered Vic.

Alexander didn't mind. It seemed only right that Vic should be nasty till the end. When he went off on his motor-bike, Alexander even waved him goodbye.

Afterwards Carol cheered up a bit and Alexander asked her to tell him about the mongooses in Africa and whether they really did kill the snakes. She said that mongooses had been a pest at her father's hospital, that they stole the chicken eggs and made nests with the hospital sheets.

Then Carol took Alexander round the garden and showed him the snapdragons—how you could open and close their little mouths. Alexander crouched on the edge of the lawn and made dragon noises and Carol held the flower between her finger and thumb and opened and closed the flower, making it gape or purse its lips. Alexander stroked Carol's smooth brown knees, as he had seen Vic do. But she pushed his hand away and stood up quickly, brushing down her skirt with both hands. Then he saw how desperate the situation really was, how Vic had made Carol hate him.

That night he dreamt about Vic. He dreamt that Vic was already in the coffin with his lank oily hair combed flat and his hawk's nose sawing the air. Alexander and Carol were dressed in black and looked a handsome couple. Alexander was standing on a chair, so he could put an arm around Carol's shoulder. Mrs. Kendal was explaining how butterfly cakes tasted so much better if you sprinkled them with icing sugar. Then the whole plate of cakes took off and began gliding about the room and the cakes unfolded like giant napkins and floated up, to dance around the light fittings. Mrs. Kendal screamed and Alexander woke up to find his mother dusting the headboard of his bed.

There's an ambulance next door, said his mother, glancing out of the bedroom window as she ran the duster along the sill.

*

When he arrived, breathless, at Carol's door and she opened it, Alexander could see she'd been crying and a great lump came into his throat at the same time as his heart was thumping in his chest.

It was me! I didn't mean it. You won't tell the police?

What are you talking about? said Carol, as she snuffled into a handkerchief.

The poison. It was me that did it. It was in the orange squash.

I can't talk to you at the moment, Alexander. I'm a little busy.

But the funeral.

Funeral, what funeral?

The ambulance, he stammered.

The ambulance came for my Dad. He had one of his fevers and they decided to take him into Stockport infirmary, to keep him under observation. But I don't think it's serious.

Vic isn't ill?

No, he's not ill but he's gone to work in London. He's got a job in a record shop. He says he's not coming back to Stockport.

She burst into a flood of tears.

*

Alexander's mother was sitting on the settee in the living room. On her knee lay an opened letter and he recognized the pale blue airmail envelope with the colourful stamps.

She looked up as he came in but, although she looked straight at him, she didn't seem to see him. Her grey eyes were dry and cold.

Bastard, was all she said and she crumpled the thin sheets of paper and they fell with an almost inaudible scuffing onto the hearth rug.

He went to her and tried to climb onto her knee but she fended him off with her elbow.

Go next door and find Carol, she said. You can play round there this afternoon, can't you?

*

After he had knocked on the front door and tried the back door and got no answer, Alexander crept into the garage next door through a broken panel he'd found. It had been so long since he had seen the rabbit that he'd forgotten the smell of it, the sweet and sour whiff of hay and urine.

She kicked as he dragged her out of the hutch but crouched still in his arms when he held her tight against him. He could feel the throbbing of her heart and the bones of her legs, and the fur on her belly was warm and damp.

He stroked the long floppy ears and watched the network of pulsating veins.

In the dim dark back of the hutch something stirred. There was a feeble rustling in the straw. The doe stiffened in his arms. Someone was rattling the garage door.

How do you get in there? came a man's voice from the driveway.

There's a key to the padlock, see? It was Carol's voice.

There was a brief struggle on the other side of the doors. They shook backwards and forwards as though two people were locked in an embrace and one of them was fighting for possession of a key.

Alexander bundled the doe back into her hutch and flung himself under the workbench where he crouched among the wood shavings and old tins of paint.

Got it!

Don't shout! You'll scare the rabbit. She's got young ones.

I won't shout, I won't… as long as you come quiet.

Carol laughed, a kind of giggle that Alexander hadn't heard before.

The doors of the garage swung open and in the brief blinding flash of daylight, Alex saw them: Carol was wearing a new dress in lime green with pink stripes down the front. Her hair had been curled and her lips looked very red in the shocked white of her face.

If my Dad catches us here, he'll kill us.

Well, he won't, will he? He's tucked up in bed feeling poorly. And him a doctor.

Doctors can get ill too, you know.

It was Vic, in a pair of pin-striped trousers and a white shirt with a thin black strip of a tie knotted tight at the neck. His hair was combed forward into a stiff quiff.

Your old man really should get someone to have a look at the stuff in here. He could flog some of it. Vic picked up a tall vase with gilt handles.

Put that down for Christ's sake. We'll get into real trouble if he knows we've been in here.

Better be quick then.

Alexander's knees were being pricked by the woodshavings and his neck was stiff with crouching down and trying to peer past the paint tins to see what was going on.

They were standing against an old kitchen cupboard against the opposite wall. Carol was sitting on the worktop.

Vic's buttocks appeared, pale in the gloom. A single beam of sunlight pierced the darkness. It illuminated Vic's right hand as he gripped the smooth brown knee that began to quiver and spasm.

Carol whimpered and Alexander wondered whether he should do something. He gripped a rusty chisel that he found in the sawdust but somehow he knew that he would do nothing, that he would wait, crouching under the workbench with the stench of motor oil in his nostrils, until they had finished whatever it was they were doing that seemed to involve so much agony and straining.

Finally they were still, gulping and groaning into each other's necks.

Alexander shifted his position and knelt on a nail sticking up through a piece of wood.

What was that?

What?

A cry. There's someone in here. Under that workbench.

It's the rabbit. She gets anxious. I said we should keep quiet. We should get out of here quick. I think I can hear my dad calling.

What does he want? Stupid old fart.

I should get him his tea. Will you come round tomorrow?

I may.

Do come. Her pleading tones faded as they stepped out, brushing down their clothes and patting their hair.

The garage door banged shut behind them.

Alexander crept out from his hiding place. He opened the door of the hutch and stretched his hand into the mound of hay at the back of the box. The doe hopped to one side to avoid his exploring hand and he found, with trembling fingers, the squirming bundles of fur. He stroked them gently while the rabbit scrabbled against the plywood wall. Then he latched the hutch door and left silently.

*

In the grey dusk he looked out of his bedroom window and saw Carol standing in the middle of the lawn. She wore a dress on which strange red flowers bloomed and she was carrying something which Alexander couldn't quite see. She knelt and dug a hole in the flower bed with a trowel and placed four small parcels in the hole, covering them with the sandy soil.

Goodnight, Alexander. His mother kissed him, a smooth dry peck on the cheek. She stood for a moment under the raffia lampshade on the landing and smoothed the front of her dress, touching the large buttons, just before she switched off the light he saw her turn towards him and smile into the darkness.

When he closed his eyes, the four little headless bodies were there, ranged on the straw. The disembodied heads were twitching and he leaned close to hear that they were singing in their thin voices. Their voices seemed to come from a great distance like the light of the stars and the words were sad and full of a meaning which he sensed it would take him years to unravel. He snuggled into the blankets and nestled his head in the pillows and it was not long before his breathing was slow and regular. The high voices died away softly and the stars burned.

Flaubert's Poison

The tragic heroine cramming the arsenic powder into her mouth by the handful and then waiting for death haunted him, as he lay on the sofa. The pages of the book were mottled, the edges curling. He even thought he caught a whiff of nineteenth century adultery in the peppery smell of old paperbacks. He went for long winter walks on the deserted beach, over the hills of shingle, beyond the shooting range to the eroded cliffs and the remnants of concrete bunkers that had been used to keep a look out for the Germans but now reeked of stale urine. During these walks he looked out over the turbid North Sea and thought of darkness and death.

He was lying on the lounge carpet and watching Pan's People dancing to "My Sweet Lord" when his mother came in. "You should go out and meet people," she said, sliding back the smoked glass of the cocktail cabinet, "It's no good sitting around here moping."

Next door's cat appeared outside on the window sill and reached up to scratch the pane of glass with its claws, setting his teeth on edge.

"If you go to the youth club or a disco you'll meet people and make friends," she said with a bright smile; Mrs Robson was fond of believing that she'd arrived at the solution to a problem. She poured a measure of Cinzano Bianco and smoothed the shag-pile with her foot. "You'll enjoy it once you're there." The cat reached up again, pressing its belly against the window pane to put all its force into the front claws.

The A level grades he'd got were mediocre, except for biology, and it seemed that his hopes of going to university to study French literature were going to be disappointed. Through a friend of his mother's he got a job in a fish research laboratory. His main duty was cleaning, but he was also responsible for feeding the cod that swam around in the big cold tanks under a low ceiling bisected by iron girders. He also had to make a record of the temperature in a bound log book. He did this with a green-ink pen and when he forgot he would fill the log in with made-up temperatures. Sometimes the fish swam to the surface to look at him with their mournful eyes. They seemed to be mouthing tales of longing—their dreams of the glass-green sea.

There was a girl working in the canteen called Martina who had a similar expression to the misty-eyed cod. And she'd brown crinkly hair—which he thought very Biblical.

"Yes?" she snapped, when he went to the canteen on his first day. "Can I help you?"

"Cup of tea, please."

She pushed hair back off her forehead: "You're new," she said critically. "What's your name?"

At school, boys had called him *pin-head* because his head was too small for his long body and broad shoulders. He was glad, at such times, that there was no one to stick their oar in and contradict him when he mumbled, "Kelvin."

"Would you like a doughnut, Kelvin?" She offered it because he had a hungry look. "These are stale. They were to going to be chucked out."

"Ta," he said.

While he was drinking the tea, she went round the tables with a cloth and soapy water in an old margarine container and wiped the formica, leaning across and smearing the tea stains with her bosom.

"How's the tea?" she asked as she cleared the crumbs.

"Lukewarm."

"Well?" she opened her mouth, showing the gum she was chewing. "What do you expect me to do about it?"

"Nothing, I suppose."

"Where are you working this afternoon?" she said and sucked a strand of hair that had come loose from the white cap.

"In the annex, cleaning the study room," he lied.

"Only I finish at three and I can come and bring you any of the sandwiches we don't sell."

When he'd finished sweeping out the laboratories, he slipped away to the tank room. The tank room was kept dim and cool. There was only the fizzing hum of the aerating pumps and the flicker of the water shadows on the ceiling. The place felt calm. He was able to squeeze behind one of the concrete pillars without anyone knowing he was there. He sat with his long legs tucked up against his chest, rested his chin on his knees and concentrated on the hum of the machinery.

As he walked home later, he wondered why he had felt compelled to lie to the girl in the canteen. The eyes rimmed with mascara had given him an uncomfortable feeling. "Well, I didn't want any stale sandwiches anyway," he said to himself.

The next morning at coffee time, Martina stared at him out of aggressively black-ringed eyes. "Where were you?" she said. "I looked for you in the annex. You weren't there, were you?"

"I had to work in the labs instead, sorry." He couldn't say why her eyes were so disturbing or why he had a sudden urge to run out of the canteen.

She slopped the tea in the saucer when she banged it down on the counter.

"What's wrong," she said, "don't you like me?"

He could feel the tips of his ears beginning to burn. "Sorry."

"Oh, shut up," she said.

When he was sweeping out the tank room that afternoon he heard the door open and saw a head of crinkly brown hair making its way round the side of the room.

"Thought I'd find you here, she said. She pushed him back against one of the tanks and reached up to kiss him. She laughed at his surprise, the look of startled bewilderment in his eyes.

"You didn't expect that, did you?"

"No."

When she'd gone, he looked down on the fish gliding around in their tanks. They weaved between each other, never touching except when he dropped the pellets of food in. Then, they churned the water, nosing above the surface in an effort to snatch the stuff from his fingers with their greedy silver lips.

After she'd finished her shift in the canteen, Martina

would meet Kelvin in the tank room. They kissed behind the cold aquariums and smoked cigarettes under the refrigeration unit looking through a narrow dirty window at a concrete promenade, deserted and wind-swept even though it was late June.

"We could have a house of our own," she'd say, "wouldn't you like that?"

"And a doughnut stall, we could run a doughnut stall."

"There'd always be something to eat."

Or they dreamed of the books they'd read. She'd be a painter and they'd go abroad and rent garrets and live a hand-to-mouth existence.

*

It was Dr Williams who'd got Kelvin the job in the fish labs. Kelvin came across him one afternoon sitting at his desk in the laboratory. The older man beckoned him over as he was sweeping under the benches.

"Have a look," he said.

Kelvin peered into the top of the microscope but all he saw were blurred patterns of light.

"Yes," he said. "Thanks."

"It's best to keep both eyes open and then the image is clearer." The older man gestured back to the apparatus.

This time there were silvery corrugations shot through with violet and blue.

"What is it?" he mumbled in spite of himself.

"A fish scale, magnified 100 times." The corrugations wavered almost as though the thing were living and breathing beneath the lens.

"I thought you'd be interested. I can see you're the kind

of lad who'd understand."

Kelvin was hot, his hands felt cloddish and thick.

"What we're looking for, you see, are any imperfections in the shape of the scales, any deformities." He held down a sheaf of papers with his thumb, pressing so hard that the thumb joint went white.

"Here's one," he lifted a thin glass plate, "from the Baltic. You can see those dark lines."

"They look red to me," or crimson, he thought, like crests of blood on each scalloped wave.

"You've a good eye for detail; my colour vision is failing."

Kelvin glanced for the first time at the man's eyes. From the side, they were visible behind the thick lenses of his glasses. The lids seemed swollen above the pale grey pupils. Kelvin remembered seeing Dr Williams once or twice on his cliff-top rambles with his head down into the wind, the collar of his coat turned up, an expression of intense concentration on his face as he marched along.

"What happens to the fish in the tanks here in the laboratory?"

"We keep them for a few years to monitor their growth and development. We dissect them at various stages to examine skeletal features and internal organs."

"They don't go back to the sea, then?"

Williams smiled. "That would be a waste of valuable research material."

There was a silence. Dr Williams fiddled with some of his equipment, their knees banged against each other under the desk.

"I'd better get on," said Kelvin lurching to his feet.

"Yes, you have to finish off, I suppose." He rested his hand, for a moment against Kelvin's arm, tremulously. "I'll let you go then." He spoke faintly, as if from the end of a long tunnel. "It'll be home time soon enough."

*

They were snogging in the gloom, the wet sounds of their kisses smothered by the slow hum of the aeration pump, when a faint noise made Kelvin look up.

"What's that?"

"A man, he's watching, spying on us, look."

A man was crouching, peering between the concrete pillars. When Kelvin got to his feet, the man bolted for the door but Kelvin got there first and stood with his fists clenched. It was Dr Williams.

"Leave him alone, Kelvin," said Martina coming up behind him. "He's always spying on me and trying to see down my bra when I'm cleaning the tables."

"There you are, Kelvin," began Williams breathlessly. "I was looking for you." He looked white and feeble. His hair, normally neatly combed, was sticking up in disordered tufts and his eyes flickered in the green dimness, unable to meet Kelvin's. "You see, Kelvin, there's something of the utmost importance I need you to help me with."

*

"I'll cook us a meal," Martina had said, but there was no sign of any food when Kelvin arrived at her bed-sit.

They sat together on her sofa bed, which was covered with a pilled orange blanket, and looked at a pile of discarded clothes in the middle of the floor. Martina lay back on the sofa and giggled.

"What's funny?"

"You are."

"Why?" Kelvin sat up.

"You just are."

Martina had put on a loose skirt which revealed her white legs. She was looking at him with a strange expression. Kelvin sat with his arms folded; after a while he picked up a magazine and began leafing through it.

She threw a cushion at him. "What did that old fart Williams want that was so important?"

"He just wanted me to move some boxes."

"It doesn't sound as though it was that important to me."

"No, maybe not."

Canvases and drawings were stacked against the walls, creating the impression that the room was crowded. They were all nudes in oil or pastel, crudely daubed in yellow, black and vivid green; clashing and crashing as legs, arms, breasts and faces fought for attention.

"Did you do all these?"

"Yep, what do you think?" Martina put her hands up to her hair and stroked the heavy biblical ringlets.

"Um..." Kelvin's eye was caught by a yellow face with starkly drawn eyes and something indefinable protruding from its mouth. "I don't know."

"You don't know what you think?"

"No." The paintings flashed on his retina when he blinked. It was as though they'd begun to seep in already through his pores to lodge in his mind permanently.

"You think they're bad. Most people loathe them.

Sometimes I take a knife to them myself. It's part of the creative process. You can say what you think, you know." She lay back on the crumpled blanket. "Well?"

Kelvin's knee began to tremble and he had to grip it to stop it shaking. "I'm getting a headache," he said. "Shall we get some fresh air?"

*

It was Martina's idea to go to the pub. They stood outside for a few minutes to let Kelvin get his nerve up. Someone was guffawing just the other side of the fogged window. Inside, people crushed against the bar. The men all seemed to be shouting and a woman with an immaculate hairdo pulled the pints. In a corner two old ladies sat with their heads enveloped in a haze of cigarette smoke. Kelvin had the feeling they were watching him.

The room was so crowded that they couldn't get near the bar. Then Martina spotted someone she knew at the bar and pushed towards him, dragging Kelvin behind her.

"This is Gary," shouted Martina.

"Drink?" Gary breathed beer in Kelvin's face.

"Lager and lime, for me," yelled Martina.

"And you?" Gary said to Kelvin. "What can I get you?"

"Whisky?" Kelvin murmured.

"Come again?"

"Can I have a whisky?"

The man's smile faded. "Whisky? You can get your own," he said, raising his eyebrows. "One lager-and-lime coming up."

Kelvin felt sweat break out in his armpits. He thought he heard the two ladies in the corner start whispering: "He didn't, did he?" "He did!"

He ploughed his way through to the counter: "Whisky!" he shouted at the woman.

"Eh?"

Kelvin couldn't speak.

"Spit it out!" she yelled at him.

Gary was laughing too. He winked at the two old ladies in the corner and they raised their sherry glasses.

"I'll have an orange juice," said Kelvin to the barmaid.

Gary and Martina seemed to be such good friends that Kelvin wondered whether they'd be happier if he wasn't there. After the drinks Gary invited Martina back to his flat. He scarcely glanced at Kelvin: "You can come too, if you want."

They climbed up the stairs of a guest house which had been converted into flats with paper-thin partitions and soaring ceilings. There was no heating in the flat and barely any furniture except the remains of an old bus seat which served as a couch. Cigarette ends littered the floor.

"I can't offer you tea," he said. "Unless you've got fifty pence for the meter."

They sat, watching their breath form clouds in the middle of the room.

"Well, fancy a smoke?" Gary licked his lips and looked round the room as if it was crowded and he was addressing several people and not just the two of them.

"I don't smoke, thanks," said Kelvin. "We might not stay long."

"A smoke would be nice," said Martina, as she wriggled herself into the corner of the bus seat.

Gary unsteadily rolled a cigarette on the grubby knee of his jeans, crumbling a tiny brown lump into it which looked like an Oxo cube.

Martina took a long slow drag on the cigarette and breathed out into Kelvin's face. "Try it, Kelvin, go on. Live dangerously!" and she began to laugh.

Kelvin stood up and a book fell from his pocket onto the bare floorboards.

"What's this?" Gary scooped up the tattered green and white paperback.

"It's *Madame Bovary*," said Kelvin, "by Flaubert."

"Flo-who?"

"Flaubert. He's a very famous French novelist of the nineteenth century."

"Oh yeah?" there was a long pause. "Very famous is he? What's it about?"

"It's about a girl who dreams of living a luxurious life and marrying into the aristocracy."

"Sounds good."

"It's very good actually. She ends up in a terrible…"

"Oh, it's actually very good, is it?" Gary gave Martina a sidelong glance.

"It has a tragic ending. She kills herself by swallowing arsenic."

There was a silence, then Martina and Gary burst into fits of laughter, throwing themselves back onto the bus seat and waving their legs in the air. Gary ended up sliding off the seat altogether.

"Another smoke, Martina?" Gary picked himself up off the floor

"Yeah, go on." Martina sank back into the corner of the settee and looked at Kelvin through narrowed eyes. "He likes reading, don't you, Kelvin?"

"I do as a matter of fact. I don't want to be working at the fish labs all my life."

"Like me, you mean?"

"I'll go, then," he said. Martina and Gary watched him getting his things together and carried on smoking.

"Will you be alright getting home?" he said to Martina.

"I 'spect so."

"I'll be off then."

"Bye."

Gary didn't say anything except, "Watch out for the milk bottles," as Kelvin tripped over a line of them by the door.

*

There was an envelope sitting on the breakfast table when Kelvin came downstairs the following morning.

"It's a university place," he said to his mother, "An unconditional offer."

"Oh, that's nice dear."

Kelvin took his rucksack into work with him, filled with wet towels. During the morning coffee break, when there was no one around in the tank room or the annex, he used a fisherman's landing net to scoop one of the cod out of the tank and into his rucksack. He dunked the rest of the towels in the tank water and threw them on top of the fish.

It took him about fifteen minutes to get down to the edge of the promenade where a high tide was washing at the sea wall. From the steps, he released the fish into the waves where it lay, twitching feebly for a few minutes, before it gave a flick of its tail and disappeared into the murky depths. Kelvin felt a rush of relief as he watched the fish go. It was almost as if something inside him had been released. He looked up at the laboratory buildings. It was going to be a long job to release all of the fish.

The Island

The bleeding chunks slid on the white plate. Judith pushed the meat around with a fork before abandoning it.

"What a waste," Duncan complained, "of good meat."

"I wasn't hungry."

She was inclined to wonder at her life these days; to view its strange twists and turns with a sense of detachment. It might have been someone else's life that she was appraising with a faintly critical air. And this feeling that she had of being outside of reality was made more acute when she was on holiday with Duncan, just the two of them. Perhaps, she wondered, children would have made a difference but, then again, maybe not.

*

Click, click, click. Trying to locate the source of the sound, Judith turned her head from side to side on the pillow. It was one of those peculiar little French bolsters that slid from under her head. Duncan's knees brushed the backs of her thighs. The clicking continued in the grey stillness of the room. Judith raised her head and peered round at the unfamiliar hulks of furniture. The dressing table mirror cast a steely triangle of light across the quilt. The clicking was, at times, almost as loud as someone snapping their fingers. She got up and went to the bathroom, feeling the tiles cool under her feet. A tap dripped softly in the sink but it wasn't that that was making the noise. She filled a glass with water and gulped it, standing in the bathroom.

Back under the quilt she still could not sleep. The

clicking, she supposed, was one of those beetles, buried somewhere in the timbers of the old hotel.

If I don't do anything, Judith said to herself, if I just lie here very quietly, perhaps it will go away. Then the thought came. She couldn't stop it. The thought just grew in her head, as if the seed of it had been waiting to burst open, and in a flash she saw her life, every scene of her life since she had married Duncan and closed the door on experience. What am I to do? she whispered into the darkness. At last, unable to sleep, she went to the window and opened the casement. The island showed its dark hump against the pale horizon. It loomed, massive, and Judith felt as if there was a spring coiled tightly inside her, fighting against her natural inertia, impelling her towards something. A bird called softly, an eerie cry in the night.

*

The following morning, Judith took out her binoculars to look at the distant panorama of the island. It shimmered in the heat haze, yet she saw that the cliffs rose sheer from the waves. The tiny white flecks of birds whirled above the island.

Duncan knew that there was nothing there but grey rocks and spiny plants and boredom. The boat trip was an indulgence to Judith's romantic view of the Mediterranean.

The boat attendant, a boy of sixteen or seventeen, was asleep in the bottom of his boat. He slept in the shade cast by a carefully positioned square of canvas draped over the bow. Judith couldn't bear to wake him up—he was sleeping so peacefully.

She'd seen the boy before, hanging around the entrance

to the hotel. He had one of those closed faces, his hair flopping forwards over his eyes, so that just the glitter of them was visible. The sort of boy who is engrossed in his own world—a world which Judith would never be able to enter.

"Don't wake him," she said to Duncan, "We can come back later."

"Nonsense." Duncan's lips tightened. "We booked this trip for nine in the morning. If we have to spend the morning messing about in the village, the whole day'll be gone."

"Hey, you! I booked this boat. Remember?"

The boy's eyes flickered.

"Go to island? Nine o'clock? Yes?" Duncan jabbed at his watch, "Nine, nine!"

Then the boy was sulkily awake. He moved slowly around the boat, tidying a coil of rope, spreading cushions on the seats. Judith watched the shadows of the water rippling on his brown arms.

How impatient Duncan could be sometimes, she thought. His sharp tones intruded on the blue and gold of the morning light. But it was a voice that smoothed the way in so many daily transactions. It was so familiar and comforting to her. She couldn't imagine life without it. Once, when Duncan had gone abroad for a sports' event, she had looked forward to being on her own for a few weeks. But she found the loneliness had been too much. The silence had sucked her up.

The boy pushed off from the quayside and the sudden violent motion made Judith's stomach turn.

"What is it?" said Duncan. "Are you OK?"

"Nothing, just the rocking of the boat makes me feel a bit sick."

"Poor Judith." Duncan reached out to touch her bare shoulder. She wished he hadn't because the boy noticed it. His quick eyes saw everything and his nostrils twitched; Duncan was a large man who smelt of sweat even after a shower. The smell of the changing rooms hung about him; the faint cheesy odour that could never quite be masked by deodorant and charcoal in-soles.

Judith sat on a piece of folded sail, trailing an arm in the warm sea, watching the boy rowing. Through her green-tinted glasses, she saw that his forearms were quite smooth and caught the silvery effect of the ripples. She imagined catching his eye, and smiling. The tiny muscles in her lips twitched, in sympathy with the idea. She was shocked by the sudden desire to be ravished, on the faded biscuit-coloured canvas, by the boy.

Duncan sat frowning at the view, eager as a spaniel. Judith felt hot with shame; she pressed her legs together and narrowed her lips to a thin steely line, so that the boy wouldn't catch her looking at him.

The island loomed above them. Duncan was out of the boat in a flash, oblivious to wet shoes and trousers. He took hold of the rope and began to haul the boat towards the shore.

"Five thirty, half past five, yes?" Duncan was saying to the boy as he helped Judith out of the boat, "You come back five thirty."

The boy was nodding and smiling. "Yes, yes."

Judith smoothed her skirt down. The way the boy's gaze flicked away when she looked round amused her—such a young boy. Then, at the last minute, he gave her a sudden brilliant smile. Judith blushed and rushed away up the path that wound up the cliff out of the bay.

"Why do you think he'll understand better if you speak to him in pidgin English, Duncan?" she said as they struggled upwards. "I'm sure he understands quite well enough." As they climbed they dislodged stones that fell with a sharp crack like pistol shots.

"I was just making sure he understood." Duncan poked at a tuft of pale grass clinging to a rock.

The boy still stood on the beach looking up at them, shading his eyes.

"Hasn't he gone yet?" Duncan stopped and eased his back for a moment.

"Maybe he's going to wait for us."

"But I just explained—that wasn't the arrangement."

"No."

They arrived at an arid plateau at the top of the cliff and saw that the boat had disappeared from the bay.

"We need some shade," said Duncan with hateful practicality, but there were no trees, only a few stunted shrubs with leaves that rattled in the breeze.

The sea was all around them, Judith saw. As if she was a bird soaring overhead, part of her could see the pair of them stumbling across a barren rock, watching them wander along a narrow path.

"I don't like this place," murmured Judith at last. "It smells of death…"

"It's probably a dead goat or something." Duncan sounded husky in the dry heat. "Or the last boatload of nature-lovers abandoned with no food or water."

A tiny lizard ran across the path and paused, turning its eye on her, a nondescript woman struggling through the tangle of bushes. It lives here—she said to herself—and we are just passing through. She considered the creature's ageless presence; it was, like the rocks, intimately connected with the island, with the harshness of existence. It made her feel silly and pointless.

"Oh," said Judith suddenly standing dead still.

The crust of ashen rock fell steeply away. Below them the sea shivered, as unreal as a great cut gem of aquamarine with shifting purple depths. The path led down to a bay of grey pebbles.

"Be careful," said Duncan. "It's steep!" But Judith was already stumbling down the path, clinging to the bare branches of plants as she went. She didn't care that the twigs scratched her shins; she was so desperate to reach the shore.

It was easy to forget about the grey plateau, smelling of goat carcasses, once you were by the sea. There was no sound in the bay except for the soft slippery sound of the waves and the frail piping of a bird from somewhere among the rocks. Judith spread her towel on a patch of sand and set up her sunshade—a thin jacket draped over two sticks. She unpacked a cushion and the book she'd been carting around.

Duncan wandered off along the shore. On the way down the path he'd seen in the sea a shape, moving in the depths, which he thought he might see better from the spit of sand that thrust out from the far side of the bay. It was such a small inlet that he thought it would be no more than a fifteen-minute walk, but, as he picked his way along the shore, the boulders which had looked small from above, now proved almost as big as houses and it was hard to find a way through.

For an hour, Judith struggled with her book. It was a clever book; almost, Judith suspected, a little too clever. In the heat, the words trailed off like insects and she found her eyelids drooping. If only she could get to the next line—but the letters clustered together. She didn't like to feel defeated, but the grey details were exhausting on such a hot day. She let the book rest on her stomach, just for a moment, and adjusted the cushion. A warm salty breeze blew softly across the sand, and Judith slept.

*

At the end of the sand spit, Duncan climbed up onto a rock to look down at the shape—whatever it was. The water lapped glassily at the rock. The dark form seemed to wave fins and he wondered whether it might be a turtle browsing on the algae. He peered closer. The formless thing seemed to swell and shrink in the depths as if it had its own pulsating life. It could have been no more than the effect of light falling through the water giving the illusion of movement but Duncan was sure he could make out the ridges and grooves of a turtle's shell.

A turtle browsing on the seaweed—his mind leapt at the idea.

The object wavered, it seemed to recede, to grow

smaller and less dense, almost as if it was transparent and he could see the pebbly depths through it. Then it surged towards the surface, flecked with silver. He thought there might have been glimmering eyes to it. Then he saw what it was: a large sheet of black plastic with ragged edges. It had been caught on the rocks and drifted to and fro with the current. A breeze ruffled the surface of the water and Duncan shuddered in spite of the heat and raised his eyes to the sky. Clouds smeared the horizon; strips of cirrus cloud were drawn out like ribs across the haze of blue and suddenly the smell was there again—the rancid smell of something long dead and festering in a ravine.

*

Judith opened her eyes with a faint sense of nausea. Something had woken her: the sharp echo of a sliding pebble. She sat up and looked up at the cliffs but there was no one. The bird was still piping somewhere among the rocks.

"Hello? Duncan, is that you?"

The bird called again, more urgently. Judith stood up to see if she could catch sight of it. She thought she saw a flutter of wings and was reaching for the binoculars when pebbles crunched behind her and she span round. The boy stood a few yards away, shading his eyes with one hand.

"Oh, it's you. I thought you were Duncan." Judith laughed. It was funny to be alone on the beach with the handsome boy.

"Look!" He held out his closed hand to her. When he opened it, she saw on the palm a tiny quivering insect. What was it? A grasshopper, she thought. It wasn't something you did: show people such things as grasshoppers. It made her giggle; a helpless gulping in her throat when he reached out to touch her breast.

There was something opaque about the eyes that were fixed on her breasts. He was very tall and older than she'd thought. His jaw had a prickling of stubble.

The boy drew back his arm suddenly and she flinched, closing her eyes for a moment.

"Please, no," she said.

He flung the insect he'd held high into the air and it buzzed away towards the cliffs.

*

The bay curved slightly and Duncan picked his way over boulders so that soon he was out of sight of Judith and her towel. He was drawn on by the irresistible impulse to see what was round the next headland. He clambered on for an hour or more, aware that time was passing but unable to turn back.

He stumbled over a lip of rock and was brought up hard. The thing was laid out on the shore. At first he only saw the alien bulk of it: the gravid curves, the streaks of paler, bluer flesh; the belly as taut as a barrel. Then there was the head, with two grinning rows of tiny pointed teeth.

Something had gouged out the eyes; only the snout was left untouched. A fin stretched, paddle-like, onto the sand as if it had tried, perversely, to haul itself out of its element. Flies whirled—a vortex of tiny devils—clustering and settling back on their sumptuous feast. It was the pale belly that he couldn't drag his eyes from, and the grin. The tail with its sweeping flukes waved in the water, surging back and forth with the bottle tops and polystyrene chips.

He couldn't take his gaze off it. The eyeless head nodded at him. Something had begun to scrape away at the creature's flanks—opening a ragged wound.

The air hummed with flies and seaweed popped on a rock. The pristine gulls wheeled above, buffeted by the thermals. They swooped down above Duncan's head and soared again, fixing him with the beads of their eyes. If it had been him opened to the sky, his entrails exposed; they would have shown no mercy. The birds settled, squabbling over some plump gelatinous morsel, oblivious to Duncan's presence. "Hey!" he shouted, and waved his arms. The birds flapped up resentfully but edged back after a few moments. Duncan felt stupid, shouting at the wildlife, so he left them to their meal and began the long return journey.

*

Judith touched the boy's shoulders, the scapular, the folds of his ears, and felt a hot flush rising from her feet, travelling up her body. She ran a finger down his cheek. He said nothing but looked mournful. Then they knelt awkwardly on the stones. The grey nodules pressed themselves into Judith's thighs and buttocks as he crouched over her, fumbling with the zip of his shorts. She repeated to herself that this was what she'd wanted, to have this boy.

At first he'd kept his eyes closed. But she was determined to claw her way into the thick-skinned boy, to make some lasting mark. When she dug the points of her nails into his back, his gaze sharpened to a resentful fury that she found herself grateful for.

The boy entered her with a hurried clumsiness. Judith

arched her pelvis in an attempt to connect with him and to force him to slow his thrusts. She was enjoying the weight of his body pressing down on her and the sight of his face framed by the curling mass of his hair that seemed to flare with the light behind it. She felt alive; he was demanding something of her that she was able to give and she felt a fierce joy.

Then came the hot swollen gush of him between her thighs and she gasped with the intensity of her pleasure, a pleasure which caused her whole body to tremble. She became vividly aware of the glittering sea and the sky; it was as if she'd been released into a fresh world which shivered with colour and light. Even the pebbles seemed smoother and her flesh experienced the pressure of each probing nodule with a new acceptance.

*

The slime of seaweed slipped underfoot as Duncan came in sight of the bay and Judith—a distant pale blur. He was anticipating the coconut smell of Judith's sun-screen, her voice raised an octave: "Where on earth have you been?"

But Judith merely lifted her head from her novel and smiled. He couldn't see beyond the green lenses of her sunglasses.

"You're back." When she pushed up the sunglasses he could see that her eyes had shrivelled to wizened raisins. Something was wrong, but Duncan could never quite fathom his wife's moods. She might just be angry that he'd been gone for such a long time.

"Did you have a sleep?" asked Duncan.

"I tried. I dozed for a little. Did you see anything on

your walk?"

"Oh, nothing much." Duncan licked a drop of sweat from his upper lip. "There's nothing much to see."

"You must have gone right round into the other cove."

"Yes." He paused, panting in the dry air. "But it's all the same, just sand and … and rocks. No sign of that boy then?"

"Not a thing. I should think he's waiting in the other bay where he brought us in. I'll just put my things together, shall I? And then we can go back."

Duncan followed the gently sloping beach down to the water. There in the wet sand he saw the marks of a boat's keel where it had been hauled out, the freshly impressed pattern of a rope and footsteps where someone had trodden.

"Are you ready, dear?" called Judith.

"Of course." Duncan turned to his wife and smiled. "Lead on," he said.

Spadework

I'm in the middle of digging a hole for a gatepost; down and dirty with a trowel and with damp patches at my knees, delving into the Norfolk clay, hacking away with a cold chisel and a hammer borrowed from my father. The old gate-post had rotted away and could be pulled out, it seemed, like a bad tooth from its socket but the part below ground didn't rot, it has remained intact, squeezed tight into the hole dug for it. The underground part of the post doesn't rot, my gardener neighbour explained, because there's no air: it's the mixture of air and water that helps the process of decay. He understands the science of it; to me it's just an awkward stump.

At the age of seven or eight I became stuck in a hole—a telegraph post hole, or a drainage hole, we never knew which—in the middle of a ploughed field. My brother was furious with me for sitting in the hole with my knees up against my chest. He told me to stop messing about and get a move on, or he'd leave and go home without me.

I was tempted to tell him to get lost, just to see what he'd do. Then I discovered I was wedged tight in the hole, unable to move, even if I'd wanted to—in the middle of a ploughed field in Norfolk with nothing to look at except the horizon and the flat, bare sky.

Last year I went to the doctor with a small lump on my lower eyelid. The doctor referred me to a consultant at the hospital, who prodded it and examined it. They sliced it off and carried out a biopsy and announced that it was a small tumour and that they would have to do more work, more gouging. It was the kind of tumour, they said, that was like a rogue ulcer that would, if unchecked, begin to burrow in.

In the newspaper, coincidentally, I'd recently read an article about a woman who'd had a tumour removed from her cheek. They'd had to remove more than they'd thought. In the end they'd had to cut away most of the right side of her face: the right eye and most of the upper jaw, leaving her with a gaping hole (there was a photograph). The left eye, clear and rather beautiful, peered out of the untouched half of her face, a pleasantly confident face.

You could only marvel at how someone could continue to exist like that with half of her face missing, leaving a black hole with cleanly healed edges. Couldn't they have done something with plastic surgery, I wondered, to cover it up? There was a complicated patch that she sometimes wore to disguise the absence but she'd taken to going out without it, the latticework of her cheek bones exposed. She'd recovered after a long period of depression and now she plays in an orchestra.

In the event, the hospital decided not to operate further on my tumour. The consultant said that the biopsy had probably removed all of the cancer cells.

But it gave me a small scare, the thought of the gouging I'd escaped, which got me to thinking that, if my brother hadn't called the fire engine out to rescue me from the hole in the ploughed field, I'd never have made it this far; I'd have sunk down into the hole, unable to move my legs or arms. The hole, which was about five feet deep, was hundreds of yards from the nearest road, a tiny country lane, out of sight in a dip of land. I'd have sunk deep, covered in layers of silt; maybe I'd have been preserved like one of those prehistoric bog-people with leathery skin and tattered scraps of cloth or perhaps I'd have been transformed into a tightly folded skeleton, to be discovered years hence and mistaken for a ritual burial, evidence of a dark cult that buried its victims alive.

So, back to the hole I'm digging, scraping away with a trowel—I'm reminded that the man who sank the original gatepost was a Norfolk bricklayer who committed suicide not long afterwards. This might have been his last job— ramming my gatepost home. There was something earthy about him, like honest clay. His hands were large and the fingers were blunt, good for moulding mortar and plaster. He'd been a good builder in his younger days but had fallen on hard times and was reduced to picking up odd jobs. He was quietly spoken and had one of those pleasantly nondescript faces, unremarkable except for the eyes. He had greeny brown eyes but he wasn't good at making eye contact, except for the last time we'd met, passing each other on Dove Street, when he'd held my gaze, turning his head to stare after me as he disappeared.

In the bottom of the hole that I've dug I can see the orange wood, like the tuberous root of a carrot. I feel slightly despairing. It's going to be a tough job to extract the remains of the post, splintered as it is by my efforts. The remains could go down another eighteen inches compressed by concrete, the concrete that my builder chap mixed up and pressed into place, smoothing it out with a trowel or with his own fingers.

I lie on the ground to try and get my cold chisel against the edges of the hole, trying to hack away a bit more of the concrete but the chisel just judders and slides down the edge of the concrete. I try breaking up the post by hammering the chisel into the wood and levering but all that happens is that the chisel gets jammed in the wood and I have to lever it free with a screwdriver.

The woman with a hole in her face said that she lay for days in a darkened room, that she stopped washing or taking care of her appearance. Then one day she realised that no one would come to rescue her from this hole and that unless she went out and faced the world she might as well give up the ghost. Having made up her mind about her future, she went out and bought some new clothes and joined an orchestra and never looked back.

My builder was unable to climb out of his depression. The voices, he said, came from inside his television. He threw a brick at it and smashed the screen. I imagined him sitting among the shards of glass looking at the empty box. He felt better, he told me, for smashing the television.

My hole hasn't got any deeper—I've reached an impasse. I've considered getting a pair of heavy duty pliers or a barbed harpoon-type contraption to yank out the remaining wood but I've got a feeling that what I really need is a much bigger hole. I've thought of hiring a Polish labourer: one of the young blond men with their clear skin and blue eyes and their expressions of incongruously cloddish resignation. There are practically no Norfolk labourers anymore. The clever young men are going into IT or the financial sector; the less clever (or perhaps the cleverest of all) are content to claim their dole cheques and sit watching the vast skies revolving over the fields of ploughed stubble. They've no intention of cleaning potatoes or bagging up Brussels sprouts, much less digging holes for a living.

Having done more extracting with a trowel, I stare down into the hole I've made and measure the depth for the umpteenth time: ten inches. The cold chisel is now useless as I can no longer get the hammer down to bash it. It's taken me two hours to dig a ten-inch hole. I'm sweating like a pig and the clouds are gathering, plum-coloured, and pregnant with rain. I'm going to give up in a minute. The shards of wood look more and more like the root of something.

Norfolk hedgerows, the majority of them, were dug up in the fifties or sixties, rooted out for intensive cultivation so that the combine-harvesters had room for manoeuvre. The little fields were transformed into endless expanses of clay. You could lose yourself in the middle of those fields. You could scream and shout and there'd be no one to hear you for miles.

It was very quiet in the middle of that field where I was stuck waiting for my brother to bring help; silent apart from the sound of my own shouting and wailing.

And then there was a moment, once I'd cried and shouted myself hoarse, when I found myself listening to the wind soughing across a field of ploughed stubble. That was all except for a distant crow hopping across the furrows. It seemed pointless to cry when there was no one to hear me. In that moment I felt as much a part of the field as if I'd been a nodule of flint. The clay surrounded me, unsentimental and unyielding. I was there for good and all it seemed for those few minutes. And since I was powerless I subsided into a kind of dreadful peace. Then with something of a jolt I slid down another inch or so. The clean rim of the horizon disappeared and I tasted grit and was reminded of the possibility of being lost, buried in a field, where no one would find me alive or even, perhaps, dead. The thought stirred me to another bout of panic under the bone-white sky.

They came at last, men with spades, to dig me out. There was even eventually a fire engine, redundant, but impressive. It took the men some time to decide how to extract me from the hole. I remember the wait and then the way the clay suddenly gave up its grip and I broke loose.

You'd think it would have given me nightmares being stuck like that. Strangely, I don't remember any. It's only later in life that bad dreams have begun to trouble me: dreams plagued by carrots—ugly chunks of carrot like the roots or stumps of gateposts; blunt fingers stained by nicotine; a green-eyed man passing me in the street and turning to have a final look; a look I've never forgotten. His hole, the one he'd perhaps been sliding into all his life, is clear to me now. He couldn't go out and buy some new clothes and join an orchestra, his hole was too deep and confining.

Finally my neighbour comes to my rescue with a massive iron pole that turns out to be perfectly designed for extracting gateposts. I'm dreading the other gatepost, for of course there are two, one on either side. After the struggle with the first one I'm expecting a tough day's work. But, after breaking through a plug of concrete at the surface, I find that the post is set in sand. That builder must have been in a hurry to get the job finished.

The clay of Norfolk sticks. You've only got to walk across a ploughed field to know that it has a glutinous clinging quality that makes it difficult to shake off. And they say that people who make their homes here find it hard to leave.

The Norfolk builder who sank my gatepost succeeded in escaping from his earthly element, his suicide was a feat of aerial grace. He hurled himself from the top of a tall building and thereby escaped briefly, elegantly, from the earth, but it was the paving stones that killed him, flying to meet him.

The Rope

The summit of a low hill was the highest point from which to look out over the forest. As she turned, Fortunata's gaze did not fix on any particular detail in the wilderness; rather she absorbed the impression of unbroken green. Not so many years before, she might have walked for days under the tree canopy and never have come to a barrier greater than a smooth brown river, sliding under the cohune palms. The loudest sound that the girl could hear was the throbbing warble of the oropendola bird: *glug glug glugglug glug loog loog loog,* like water draining from a bottle, and the zither-like rustle of its wings as it hung upside down, suspended from a branch and cocked its head quizzically. Her mind revolved in the space inside her skull, curling like a small animal, soft in its silence. She turned away from the view finally and made her way back to a small hut in a clearing in the trees.

"Fortunata," said Mamita when she came home, "go to Barbosa's store on the highway and sell the plantains and pineapples that grandma has been growing in her garden and bring back a rope. It's something we'll need for our journey." Mamita had been away for a week working to earn the precious disks that buy the corn; she looked tired and her face was as empty as a freshly-scraped cooking pot.

"If you see the men, stand still. Don't move, don't look. Whatever you do, don't look in their eyes and if they speak to you, pretend that you didn't hear, that you're as deaf as a snake."

"Where are you off to—can I come?" her brother Francisco asked from his seat in the shade.

"Barbosa's store: I'm going to sell the plantains. You'll never make it that far. How can you?" Fortunata slung the plantains into a sack.

Francisco massaged his useless leg which was twisted out of shape and pulled a face. Then, he went back to his game of squashing the ants that were climbing up the legs of his chair.

Fortunata set off with the sack of plantains and two pineapples. And the oropendola bird fanned its tail in the sunlight and watched her go.

Mamita worked in the mining village. She poured wine for the men who went down into the ground. They went down the wooden shafts, so far down that their faces of burnished copper were invisible, unless someone lit a cigarette.

The mines went deep. When it rained, the gushing waters opened up the shafts and tore open the earth creating a pit of mud. Already there was a canyon, so wide you couldn't see the other side when you stood on its rim. Sometimes the miners came back from their labours with hard lumps of the yellow stuff. They smiled then, and drank and laughed until they choked with tears and wanted *jiggy-jiggy* and Mamita sat on their bellies and played with them. Mamita smiled her empty smile and thought of the luxuries she'd be able to buy with all the disks she earned. But sometimes, especially when it rained, they came back with faces like thunder clouds and they beat Mamita. Sometimes they stroked her; sometimes they slapped. Usually it was all the same to Mamita, but lately the miners had been losing a lot of over-time and they had to take it out on someone.

Sao Tomas, the nearest town, used to be a quiet place at night: it was always the same—what was there to be excited about? When they brought electricity to the town, everyone knew that things would change forever. The blue flame jumped out of the wires and lit up the streets with coloured lights in the trees and people came from far and wide to sing and dance the latest tunes. That was the great thing about electricity, it turned the greys and browns and the endless stodgy green of the forest into an explosion of colours.

They put up tall poles and strung out the black wires like vines and the blue flame came along the wires, flickering its blue tongue like lightning. Soon the store had a freezer and a TV set. Papita sat in the bar and found it was good to drink cold beer and watch slim girls with no hips at all, sitting on couches and talking in a funny foreign lingo. As he watched the ladies he wondered what kind of a life it was where you sat by a blue pool all day and did nothing except sip something from a tall glass. He forgot about his cocoa pods and they fell and rotted in the orchard.

Now that there was the blue flame in the wires and cold beer, you could sit in the bar all day clinking ice and falling off the bar stools. There was a tiredness in Papita's limbs. It was hard to get to the orchard and, anyway, the cocoa pods sold cheap these days.

And one day Papita went to Sao Tomas and failed to come home. So, Fortunata was on her way to Barbosa's to buy a rope. In red or blue or metallic purple, any colour as long as it wasn't green. She was going to buy a strong rope, stronger and better, longer and more supple, than anything that could be made in the village.

She stopped by a stream to taste the slow brown water. The surface of the water fizzed with mosquito larvae that she sieved out with her lips as she drank. A snake, patterned in bands of pink, yellow and black like a bracelet, paused as it slid through the tangled heliconia and ferns, when it saw another had come to drink.

"I'm off to the store to buy a rope," said Fortunata to the snake.

"What for?" enquired the snake, edging a little closer.

"Because we are leaving the forest," replied the girl.

"Stay here," invited the snake, peering at the girl with its lidless eyes. It had existed in this place for over two hundred thousand years, in one form or another, and saw no reason to be anywhere else.

Fortunata watched the snake coiling itself into a tight knot in the undergrowth, mesmerised by the colours and the banded pattern. Once, according to her grandmother, there had been a god in every leaf. There had been the god of the stepping stones and another god in the old mango tree before it was chopped down to make way for the electricity and the wide black road; there had been a god of the river and a god of rain drops.

She felt a sudden lethargy take possession of her limbs. The rope in her mind turned into a snake that slithered off into the undergrowth.

She woke to the song of the oropendola like gurgling

water. Her grandmother had often told how the bird weaved its basket nest. It was the oropendola that, in the beginning of time, weaved the rope by which the spirit of the sun climbed up to heaven to bring back the light which had been stolen by his jealous brother the moon. And it was the oropendola which took care of the souls of dead men, weaving a basket of light to take them up to heaven. Mamita had been angry when grandma told these stories. "How can you fill the child's head with such rubbish!" she'd complained. But the song of the oropendola bird made even Mamita prick her ears.

It was pleasant to lie in the sun by the pool and for a time Fortunata was content to be a part of the stillness around her, but finally she shook herself: "I have to go," she said firmly.

She walked across the bridge made of old railway sleepers. There was a railway once that took away the massive red logs and brought orchid hunters wrapped in clouds of white muslin to keep out the flies. Now nothing of the railway remained, except the mouldering bridge and the vague outline of an embankment by the river.

Uncle Mathias had been so good at shinning up the trees to fetch down the clusters of flowers, with leaves and roots intact, that he earned his family a small fortune until he fell and broke his neck. Still, Emilia, the eldest, married a store-keeper from Sao Cristobal and now lived in a glass castle somewhere in the city. No one remembered what she looked like.

Mamita wanted to live in a glass castle. She wouldn't make corn cakes; she would have the food *'sent up'*. She told Fortunata this and Fortunata was convinced, though she hadn't quite formed in her head a clear idea of Mamita's castle of desire.

The forest was growing dark. The sweet sour sickly blackness sucked everything into itself. The girl wrapped herself in one of the great leaves that grew out of the river bank. The rain hissed down, but in the crook of the leaf she was dry except for a thin trickle of rain worming its way down her spine. One day she would live in a room like a tent made of light and the rain would never seep in, but for now she'd be content with the leaf.

The following morning she continued threading her way through the thinning trees; there were fewer and fewer big trees now and it became more and more difficult to shelter from the sun. From time to time she passed small-holdings, each one with its hedge of thorn bushes.

On a narrow stretch of the path, the men came marching past. She froze when she saw them, still as the dead branches, not moving a muscle. "Stand still," Mamita had said, "Don't move, don't look. Whatever you do, don't look in their eyes and if they speak to you, pretend that you didn't hear."

As the men strode past, Fortunata could feel the heat of their bodies and her nostrils twitched at the rancid smell they carried with them but she stood stock still. One man stopped and his boots shuffled in the dust in front of her downcast eyes.

"I can smell pineapples. Is it pineapples you've got?" He dropped his cigarette and ground it into the dirt with his heel. "D'you want to sell me your pineapples?"

Fortunata's eyes flickered but she said nothing. Then the man laughed loud and raucous: "Someone's cut out her tongue!" And he swung back into line.

When they had gone, she crept forwards again and, finally, she arrived at the road. Her feet were sore with walking along the hard soil of the forest tracks.

*

Barbosa's store had everything that was to be had: table cloths and wall clocks and electric lamps full of oil that glittered when heated up, boxes that snapped shut and tall pink plastic tumblers. There was always a stack of coiled ropes and basins in all colours.

There were some things—the white powders and little oval beans like drops of dew—which he kept locked away in the tall cabinet in the back of the store. You needed a lot for the those things; more than most people could afford. If your head ached, as though a hammer was chipping away at your skull, the white powder or the glass bean would take away the pain. It was magic and those who had taken the powder said it was like being surrounded by a cold white light, as though all the ice cubes in the world had been crushed up.

Barbosa stood at the back of his store in the shade watching for customers. He slipped a piece of ripe mango into his mouth. It slithered there for a moment until he sucked it down, amber juice oozing from the corner of his mouth. He watched the girl as she ran her hands over the plastic basins and the coils of rope. He'd seen her before: a 'bugre', a poor urchin from up the valley with no shoes and a grubby shift. He didn't mind. He put down the mango he was peeling and called to her.

"What you want missy?"

"A rope."

"You have money?"

"No, but I'm going to sell the pineapples and the plantains."

"Ah," said the storekeeper. "But you'll never have enough for one of those ropes. Show me your plantains."

She unwrapped the contents of the sack. The pineapples smelled over-ripe and the plantains were getting black and squashy.

"No one will give you a cent for this load of shit," he said kindly.

He stroked his knee and looked at the girl for a long time in silence.

"Listen. I'll sell you a rope. You just give me the plantains and the pineapples and come to the back of the store and show me how you can do *jiggy-jiggy* and we'll call it a deal.

"And two pink tumblers. I'll throw in two pink tumblers," he added. He was a handsome man, according to his friends, with a generous heart and a fine moustache. His eyes were shiny and black, like pebbles in the stream bed. He tried to be very gentle because that's the kind of man he was.

*

As she emerged from Barbosa's store, Fortunata saw a bird flutter up into the tree growing in the forecourt. The oropendola sang in the top of the tree at such a pitch that Barbosa came out to take a shot at it with his gun but the wily bird just settled higher in the dense foliage and carried on singing.

"Those damn birds," he cursed as he pulled his shirt straight over his plump belly. "That song's enough to drive a fellow mad. Now, off you go missy." He helped Fortunata shoulder her burden and slumped in the shade of the porch with a bottle of beer.

So she set off back home with a long nylon rope, braided blue and yellow—two colours for the price of one. The tumblers rattled around in a white plastic bag. She scurried along the side of the road as a lorry lumbered by and a bright yellow bus with people hanging out of the doors, yelling.

She found the forest track again where it joined the road and began the long journey back to the village. The white plastic bag hit her ankles as she walked and became muddied. The thorns of trailing vines caught at the smooth material and small tears appeared in the sides of the bag, but she carried her booty past the old bridge made of railway sleepers and the remains of the mango tree; all the way along the looping black wire.

The sweltering insect-scratched darkness came down but she knew the path so well that she carried on walking. She paused to drink at the pool with the stepping stones but there was nothing to see except the shuddering starlight.

It was full morning when she appeared at the door of the hut, clutching the tattered bag. Mamita greeted her with a rare smile and put out a tired hand to stroke her hair. Fortunata thought of the man in his store and wanted to tell Mamita everything that had happened, but the words fluttered and died in her throat.

Mamita made corn cakes with the last of the maize, rolling the paste between her palms and smiling a strange elastic smile that stretched like the maize dough.

As Fortunata and her brother Francisco finished their meal, Mamita assured them that one day soon they would live in the city in a tent of light.

"Yes," she reiterated, securing one end of the rope to the strong roof beam, "there will be no more need of corn cakes and the hut with the broken furniture."

Mamita looked through the loop of rope at them and her eyes glittered: "We'll all live together and never do any more work."

"How?" asked Fortunata.

"How?" A small frown disturbed Mamita's smooth forehead but, before she could answer she was interrupted by the rustle of wings.

The oropendola bird, which all the time had been watching from the branches of a tall ceiba tree, fluttered down and perched in a bush next to the hut. It rattled its wings and turned itself upside down for a better look into the interior of the dwelling.

Mamita had made a noose out of the loose end of the rope and placed it around the slender neck of her son. She was about to haul the crippled child aloft but, when she saw the bird, she paused for a moment in her work, staring up at the creature which was observing her intently. "I hear you," she said as she hauled on the rope. She hauled up Fortunata next to her brother, sweating with the effort and finally, when her daughter's legs had ceased kicking, she stood up on the rickety little table, tightened the noose around her own neck and swung from the sturdy roof beam.

Meanwhile the oropendola soared into the air. The feathers of its wings spread like fingers in the fractured light. There was a commotion inside the hut—a crashing and thrashing and all the time the bird swept to and fro above the hut with a rush of wings, singing. As it flew, streaks of light began to materialise and the pouring out of its liquid song grew louder and louder until it drowned out the last feeble cries. The threads of light and the phrases of the bird's song weaved into each other to create a glimmering pulsating cable that bound up the limp occupants of the hut and drew them upwards into the sky. The song became fainter... *glug glug loog loog loog...* like the last dribblings from a bottle lying on its side.

The eyes of Fortunata looked down at the hut with its roof of palm leaves as she was swept up. Eventually, when she was no more than a confused dot above the sea of leaves, silence returned to the hillside with the view across the wilderness to a faint cobalt line—the edge of the visible world.

Shell Fire

When Vernon held the crimped lip of the shell to his ear, he could hear the faint rush of the sea. It was a miracle to hear the waves distantly crashing, especially when he knew the sea was hundreds of miles away. He wondered which waves on which sea, as he turned the shell. He looked into the curling antechamber that led into the smooth interior, inserted a finger and waggled it around, wishing he were small enough to crawl inside and see what was within. He wanted to penetrate the innermost chambers of the shell, to sit in the ultimate and smallest recess. He was sure he'd be happy there. Then he pressed the shell once more to his ear to hear the sea.

In the weedy plot behind the house were snails. When he touched them gingerly, they pulled in the stalks of their eyes and sucked themselves into their homes. In winter they clung together in brittle bunches like desiccated grapes. But Vernon's shell was different: it had a flush of pinkish bronze and sometimes a trickle of coarse white sand emerged.

He still had the shell, forty-five years later, and sometimes, when he was in a good mood, he'd take it down from its shelf above the fireplace, running his fingers over the grooves and ridges.

*

Vernon Bradley threw his mop into the cleaning cupboard and tried to slam the door. But instead of the satisfying slam, the handle of the mop slipped forward and jammed in the door; then the mop and bucket fell out into the corridor, leaving suds on the parquet. When he had cleared up, Vernon took his broom and prepared himself for the job of sweeping leaves.

As he worked, he was transfixed by the way the wind whirled the leaves, drawing them into a tight cone and then flinging them up in an eddying vortex of russet fragments which were caught by the light as they turned. He leaned on the handle of his broom and watched this game of leaves and wind, the way he sometimes watched a breeze ruffling a puddle or the shapes of clouds over the playing fields. At these times it seemed that the world was made for him alone, and that these effects of nature were unobserved except by him.

He bent down and picked up one of the leaves, turning it in his fingers. He let it fall back into the pile of leaves and slowly straightened up. He began to sweep again, feeling contentment in the comfortable sound of the broom, the rhythmic motion of his arms, the contraction of his muscles.

*

The headmaster, Mr Kelly, looked out of his office window. The school playground was empty, just the acres of tarmac and the dilapidated toilet block. The caretaker was fussing in the corner with a pile of leaves. What was that man doing?

Mr Kelly tasted bile: "How long has Bradley been with the school, Miss Glacer?"

"As long as I can remember."

"He must be…" Mr Kelly examined the husk of a fly

that had died on his window ledge, "… sixty, would you say?"

"Not quite that, I don't think."

Mr Kelly shuffled a pile of papers, straightening the edges. He lined up a ruler with the edge of the pages. But he couldn't prevent his eyes flicking back to the caretaker's slow movements.

"What is that man doing?"

Miss Glacer glanced out of the window. She was thinking of succulent flakes of cold chicken, with thinly sliced gherkins. "Sweeping?" she suggested.

"Could you ask him to come in here?" Mr Kelly used a thumbnail to clean between two of his front teeth. Then he brought up the budget spreadsheet on his laptop.

Vernon was sweeping the leaves into a pile. Every time he got the pile small enough to pick up with a shovel, a puff of wind grabbed them and threw them about.

He was surprised to see the school secretary walking towards him across the playground. She was hugging her mint-green cardigan tightly around her. She walked with tight little steps as though she had to keep to a line, buttocks clenched.

"Mr Kelly wants to see you in his office, Mr Bradley, if you've a moment."

Vernon looked at her sideways, leaning on his broom. The yellowed whites of his eyes slid round.

"I'll be there directly, Miss Glacer. Directly I've finished sweeping up these leaves."

"Oh," said Miss Glacer, pulling the sleeves of her cardigan tighter against the stiff breeze, "I wouldn't worry about leaves."

"I'll come now, then." Vernon put down his broom and the leaves that he'd got together began to fly off.

But Miss Glacer's buttocks were in retreat. Her heels clicked. She'd decided that after the chicken, she'd have an individual ginger cheesecake with a square of chocolate.

*

Vernon turned the letter in his hands; eventually he set it down on the table amongst the breakfast things. While he was eating his toast he glanced at it. He didn't like the look of the letter.

After breakfast he took it round to Mrs Crabbe who always read his letters for him.

"It's a letter," said Mrs Crabbe, adjusting the frames of her reading glasses on the her nose, "from Hawksmoor Roman Catholic Middle School." She coughed and held the letter further off. "Dear Mr Bradley," she read, "due to the current round of budgetary restrictions, the school is not able to offer a renewal of all the on-going contracts for hygiene employees and given the demands of the new hygiene delivery strategy for this institution, your qualifications…" Mrs Crabbe, gave a small gasp and ran her tongue over the tips of her dentures. There was something of the lizard about Mrs Crabbe. Her narrowed eyes shuttled sideways as if she'd spotted something edible on the kitchen surface and the wattles of skin at her neck quivered.

"Oh dear, Mr Bradley," Mrs Crabbe could only give a sympathetic wince. "It looks as if you've lost your job."

"Lost?"

She licked her lips; they were so cracked and dry. "That's it, Mr Bradley, in a nutshell."

"In a nutshell?" Mr Bradley's soft brown eyes travelled down Mrs Crabbe's house-coat, its hard buttons winked like the shards of beetles.

Mrs Crabbe grasped her door handle under this scrutiny. She handed the letter back. "That's what it says." She peered out of her scaled eyes and blinked away the dust. She would go off to the mini-market presently for some water biscuits and a packet of seed for the canary. "It's these Catholic schools, if you want my opinion." She was holding the door open a crack still. "Now if it was the Evangelicals…" But he failed to catch the end of her sentence.

Back home, Vernon sat meekly in his usual chair by the window; the shadows lengthened and still he sat and a skin formed on his cup of tea. It was only now that he began to relive his humiliation: standing with his big hands dangling beyond his cuffs in the headmaster's study, looking at the trophies and framed diplomas while the man behind the desk shuffled papers. He'd begun to sweat and Mr Kelly had twitched his nostrils.

The headmaster had shown him a scrupulous politeness that, now he thought of it, stuck in his craw: "Thank you so much, Mr Bradley, for sparing the time to come and see me." Mr Kelly had said he was "a valued member of staff; one of our greatest assets." But he'd gone on about a certificate. And as he was leaving: "Oh, there's some graffiti, Mr Bradley, by the front gate. Would you be able to deal with it tonight? It's late, I know and I don't want to keep you behind but it's in a very visible area and makes such a bad impression on visitors. Would you be able to? That's excellent. Thank you so much."

Vernon realised now that he'd been fucked over, well and truly. "Yes Mr Kelly, no Mr Kelly. I'll clean your fucking graffiti off your fucking wall even though I'm working overtime for no pay!"

For thirty years, Vernon Bradley had been the caretaker at Hawksmoor Middle School. For thirty years he'd scrubbed, swept, polished and fixed; unblocked drains, gutters and downpipes; moved furniture, set out chairs, stacked chairs and cleared up after the Christmas party, kept vigil, endured... No one knew what he'd done.

Two large, unexpected tears formed; he dashed them from his eyes and began to curse everyone he could think of. When he was tired of cursing he thought he would have a drink to calm his nerves and found a bottle of rum in a cupboard that he'd been saving. He poured himself a large glass: "Congratulations on your retirement," he said to his reflection in the mirror and tossed back the rum, which burned his throat.

After the third glass he sat down on the settee and let out a resounding fart. Then he began to giggle. Old Mr Bradley, his father, was looking down from the alcove. He wore a crisp white shirt and a straw boater. He'd just arrived in England. In the photograph his black skin shone and his plump cheeks expanded to fill the frame.

"What you grinning at?" Bradley junior made a rude gesture at Bradley senior. "This fucking country you're so proud of... Never done nothing for me."

He raised his glass. "You stupid old bugger!" He knocked the bottle of rum and it emptied onto the hearthrug. Never mind, he thought, there was a case of beer in the fridge and always the off-licence.

*

Tap, tap, tap…

Vernon Bradley was bent over the low brick wall of a garden; it was the leaves of privet that he noticed, tinged orange in the streetlights. It was night. The dull yellow light made him want to howl. Someone was touching his arm. It was a slight, irritating touch.

"Bugger off!" he said in a thick voice.

Tap, tap, tap…

"Leave me alone!" He would have lashed out but had no strength. He was dimly recalling his journey back from the off-licence with the bottle of bacardi. He remembered sitting down to crack the metal seal on the bottle and taking a few large gulps. He was sweating now as he slumped over the wall feeling a powerful urge to vomit.

There it was again: that feather-light touch on the elbow.

"Don't!" He raised his arm. "Leave me alone." Because he was remembering, from long ago, the three white men.

He tried to focus on the face that wavered in front of him. It was a young face—one of the boys from the school. The blond kid who smelt of wee. What was he doing, wandering around at this time of night? The boy might have spoken but if he did the words were too thin and papery for Vernon to hear. Anyway he soon went and Vernon, using the tops of walls and the splintered rails of fences, clawed his way home.

*

She was odd, the girl in the mini-market. Vernon found her stare unsettling as he banged down the cartons of juice and milk, the loaf of sliced bread and the three slabs of cheese in their plastic wrappers.

"That all?" And she raised her eyebrows and looked so hard that he felt as though she was trying to peel back the skin of his thoughts.

"What else?"

"I don't know, do I? You don't want no fruit or nothing?"

"No."

"This all you eat?"

"Mainly."

Vernon remembered that she'd been one of the pupils at Hawksmoor School, ten or fifteen years ago. She'd had a mouth on her then and still had, by the looks of it. With her hair pulled back and the sliver of chewing gum that poked out between her lips as she spoke, the girl was making him want to rush out of the shop and back to his house. He was relieved when she began scanning his items with sulky movements, her breasts moving inside her sparkly top.

"I don't know what you want to eat this stuff for." She prodded the loaf of bread. "It's got no vitamins you know."

"It's what I eat."

"I can cook a nice meal for you." She gave a sly sideways glance as she totalled up. "I'm a good cook."

"No." He piled the stuff into a blue carrier. "I can do for myself."

"Suit yourself."

As he unlatched his front door, Vernon caught sight of himself in the hall mirror: his shabby coat, the patchy beard, the yellowing eyes. He wondered why young girls flirted like that. He imagined her sitting on his sofa, peeling off the sparkly top, her heavy breasts. He looked down at himself, at the grey flannels and baggy pullover.

"No," he said, "No, no, no," and shambled through to the kitchen. Through the back window he could see in his garden the piles of sand and cement, a trench he was labouring at, digging down through the layers of rubble into the heavy London clay. Already it was a deep trench.

*

When he was six or seven, his mother took Vernon to see the family backhome in the West Indies. He remembered how the heat crept into his clothes, glued them to his limbs and suffocated every breath; the fierce glittering sea; the sky filled with purple clouds like the bruised flesh of a prize-fighter.

He was frightened by everything: by the huge moths that battered themselves to pieces against the lamps, by the unexpected scuffling of a small grey lizard and most of all by the swarms of cockroaches that his mother tried to ward off with a slipper. He clung to the shell that Uncle George had given him, pressing its cool hard spine against his chest. It was the one thing of beauty.

And then the storm: rain falling in torrents, hammering on the tin roofs; the wind crashing into the sides of the house and things flying past: other people's fences and roofs, clothing ripped from washing lines, a cascade of orange flowers torn from a vine, a blue plastic paddling pool... and all the while the wind roaring so that you couldn't hear yourself think.

Afterwards people said it was just a small storm, nothing like what they'd had just a few years back when whole houses were seized and flung into the air and even a cow, according to his grandmother, thrown, alive, into the top of a palm tree. No, this was nothing like a bad storm.

*

Vernon was breaking up some pieces of tile in his back garden when a small voice, as frail as a reed, said: "What are you doing?" He couldn't see, at first, who was speaking and began to suspect a mental aberration when the voice came again: "What are you breaking those tiles for?" A pointed face was staring at him between the broken fence slats in one corner.

His house backed onto the school playing fields. Since Vernon had previously been on the other side of the fence he didn't realise how much of his life was visible from the school. He made a mental note to have the fence repaired and made higher.

"What are you doing there? Hey?" Vernon felt exposed. "This is private property, private, hear? You're trespassing."

"Looking isn't trespassing."

"Breaking fences," said Vernon, "is a criminal offence."

"It was already broken."

"You're too lippy, by far." Vernon began to feel more and more like his father who'd lecture boys who came round to retrieve footballs. He'd always resented his father's meanness, the way he kept people at bay, and now here he was, turning into his father. As if it wasn't enough to have got his bulbous nose, his swarthy skin, he had now to endure his father's very words crawling out of his mouth.

The small face was already withdrawing when Vernon said: "But since the fence is broken you may as well come on through."

It was the same boy he'd met that drunken night—his face still tinged, it seemed, with the glow of the street lamps. He looked at the piles of hard-core, the heaps of sand, the trench that Vernon was excavating.

"What is it?"

"A building." Vernon could say nothing more. He was afraid to reveal, even to this boy, what it was he was creating. The broken tiles, the rubble, the pieces of scrap iron. Suddenly it all looked disorganised, childish, a muddle. He felt angry with the boy for intruding in his private world. "You shouldn't be here. Don't you have lessons?"

Then he looked more closely: "What's wrong with your face? How did you get those bruises? Who did that to you?"

"I'll go now," whispered the boy.

"Wait!"

The boy looked so sullen and lost that Vernon felt compelled, in spite of his revulsion, to comfort him. His shoulders were hunched as though he'd a great weight on them. Yet, the boy's moon face left Vernon in the dark, because he could never tell what a white boy was thinking.

"What's your name?"

"Carl."

"Why don't you go back to school? You'll be late for your class."

"I want to stay here with you."

"You can't do that."

*

First were the foundations of hard-core, then the armature of steel pipes wrapped with chicken wire and coated with mortar. It was a slow process to mould the wire and press in the mortar.

The boy came to watch, hunched in a grubby t-shirt, which he pulled over his knees and down to his ankles. The bruises were more intense, a shiny purple-black against his bilious flesh. At first Vernon felt self-conscious, with those black eyes watching his every movement but, moving around, mixing the concrete and pounding pieces of hard-core he forgot about the boy. As he worked he grunted with effort—he enjoyed the blending of the sand and cement, turning the mixture with his spade and the slopping sound of the wet malleable stuff that would soon be hard and impenetrable, soon to be shaped according to his plans.

And all the time the boy followed his movements, sitting silent and still as though he'd sprouted there like a mushroom.

As the months passed, he began to assist in small ways: handing a cold-chisel or a lump hammer; the tools hung heavy from his wrists. Then he'd wander off into a corner of the garden to play some solitary game while Vernon worked on. Seeing him, Vernon was reminded of himself at a similar age...

...crouching in the tall weeds. He'd taken his shell with him; its hardness comforted. The sun was hot on the back of his neck so that he felt their shadows rather than heard or saw the approach of the men.

"It's our little nigger friend," said the tall one because he was the leader. They were smartly dressed men who wore ties. But the leader had taken his tie off. His neck was tanned above his collar. They gave him their sunny smiles, all three of them.

Then, taking him by the arms, they led him to a corner of the field, under a hawthorn that had long since shed its white blossoms. And, smiling still, they made him kneel.

"What's this?" said one, and took the shell from Vernon and tried to smash it by hurling it against a rock but the shell was strong and bounced away into the nettles.

"Get down," they said. They forced him face down into the nettles.

Some shells, according to his uncle, possess an operculum—Vernon remembered the scientific precision of the word—with which they stop up the entrance to their refuge when danger threatens. The creature could be inside, safe and enclosed. Nothing could enter in to disturb its inner peace.

When Vernon came to, he saw his own face: his forehead caved in, the eyes and lips swollen, out of proportion to the narrow jaw. It was his reflection, he realised, distorted by the curve of the empty bottle that lay by his head; the bottle they had used to beat him with. Stiffly, he got to his feet and stumbled over something lying in the weeds—his shell. At home his mother, busy with the washing, said: "Are you OK, Vernon?" And Vernon said that he was, that he'd fallen in the nettles but was all right. "Those nettles," said his mother, "you're always in the nettles."

*

One day the boy called him over. "Look." Two snails were locked together, their shells jammed close as they fought to press their glistening bodies against each other. Between them was a pulsating thread of white, binding them. There was a tiny grinding sound as the shells moved.

"What are they doing?" The boy squatted close to Vernon, his blond head almost touching.

"Mating." The snails were still. A white froth issued from between the sliding mantles. Man and boy peered close, fascinated.

Vernon started; the boy had placed a hand on his thigh close to the crotch, a subtle pressure but cold. Vernon felt the sudden chill through his jeans. As he jerked his leg away, the boy's hand drew back—a pale flash. Vernon raised his hand to strike then stopped: "You'd best go," he said. "Go on, get lost."

*

Vernon was having a peanut butter sandwich and taking thoughtful sips from a glass of milk that was slightly tainted when there was a soft knock at the door. He put down his sandwich; it was so unusual for there to be a knock at the door at this time of day that he felt a sense of unease in his stomach. He tasted the peanut butter that had glued itself to the roof of his mouth.

"Who is it?" he bellowed, loud enough to be heard in the street.

"It's me, Shazia."

"What you want then?"

"Speak with you." Her voice was faint but determined.

"I don't want visitors." Cold fingers of sweat were

tickling Vernon's armpits.

"I got something for you."

"For God's sake!" Vernon heaved himself out of his chair. As he yanked the door open, the girl from the minimarket stepped back a few feet. She looked ready to bolt.

"What is it?"

"I made this for you." She pushed a package into his hands. He shuffled to one side to let her pass. Shazia dropped her gaze and stepped through Mr Bradley's dilapidated front door, smoothing the sleeves of her shiny jacket.

She looked round the room: "People say you're building something."

"Who that?" Vernon put the package on the table frowning. "Who says I'm building anything?"

Shazia ignored the question: "It's a flat bread," she said, as if it was her duty to bring the conversation back to the important issue in hand. "I made it myself. Aren't you going to open it?" Shazia sat on one of the dining chairs and crossed her legs. Vernon's eyes followed the line of the stockings.

He peeled back the layers of paper to reveal the pale lumpy crust, dusted with flour. The room was filled with its slightly sweet fragrance.

"You like flat bread?"

"Uh huh." He touched the soft, rounded dome of the loaf and it gave under his fingers.

"What is it you're building?" Shazia's eyes were hard and shiny in the dimness.

"That's nothing for you to know." Vernon began to

gouge lumps from the bread, his fingers dug into the crust.

"Why not? Why can't I see?" She licked her lips and leaned back in the chair so that her jacket fell open. If you like, she seemed to be saying, you can kiss me.

"Because it's my private business." Vernon was stuffing the lumps of sweet oily dough into his mouth. He realised that he was hungry, ravenously hungry. He couldn't get the bread down fast enough.

Shazia turned to him. Her bottom lip was thrust out.

"I want to see," she insisted. Her eyes flicked around the room, as if searching for a bargain.

In his mind, Vernon saw it, rising in a perfect spiral, the sunlight glinting on its ridges—a great shining horn against the sky.

"It's not finished," he said.

"How, not finished?" She was growing irritable now. The painted nails curled and uncurled in her palms. "What's so special about this stupid thing?" She moved towards the door that led into the back room but Vernon caught her by the arm as she reached for the door handle.

"No."

Her hand was on the handle when he grabbed her. Her face had a startled look, as she found herself pinned to the wall, slightly winded by his abrupt force and the shock of his limbs that had the power to bend and crush her under the weight of his desire. She had no time even to close her mouth before he'd pressed his mouth into hers. He took his kiss with an angry gulping, feeling her lipstick greasy on his tongue. As he pressed back he felt the bones inside her face, behind the yielding flesh. Vernon finally stepped away and they stood panting and looking at each other.

"Come on then," she said. She shrugged off her jacket and began pulling Vernon towards the settee. She hung over him, her hair falling while he fumbled with his belt. He felt infuriated by this girl who'd forced her way in. She was unzipping him, reaching in, when he gasped as a dull pain struck him at the apex of his thighs.

Shazia stopped kneading him: "What is it?"

"Nothing," but he was limp now and pulled away.

"What's wrong with you?"

"Nothing."

"Nothing?" She stood up and began to arrange herself. "I have to go to work," she said winding her thick mass of hair into a coil and pinning it. "They don't like it if I'm late."

Soon the front door slammed, the knocker rattled and silence settled in Vernon's house.

*

Some molluscs feed by scraping at clinging plants with their jaws, others rasp at the rock itself, even burrowing in, tunnelling into the solid rock. His uncle had shown him where they'd eaten away at the stone piers of the house; soon they would start on the foundations. Other shells are parasitic, piercing the soft tissues of their host to drain out the life-blood in tiny sips. The cone shell is a predator, shooting a poisoned dart, a tiny sliver of calcium, so venomous it could kill a man. It then sucks the victim, a small fish or shrimp, into its stomach.

Shells grow by small accretions, by the layering of calcite and aragonite. It is the work of decades. As he pressed each fragment into place and smoothed the grout with his fingers, Vernon felt intensely happy. In the moulding of these ribs of glass and concrete he felt he was nudging something into place. He could have been touching flesh as he pressed and poked. The foil wrappers glinted with a sudden numinous energy in the dim light as he prodded them into position. Time was unmeasured in this coiled space—his physical needs seemed to fade. Finally, a raging hunger or thirst would come over him and he would stagger into the kitchen in search of a loaf of bread or a carton of milk to fill the space. Or chop an onion and stuff it, raw, into his mouth.

*

A staircase spiralled up inside and there were windows at intervals in the curving walls. These windows were filled with tinted glass: amber and rose and green so that walking up the stairs you were bathed in bands of colour. The spaces between the windows were formed of fragments of glass and tile embedded in concrete. The glass was from milk-of-magnesia and Seven-Up bottles and marmite jars saved over three decades by Vernon's mother under the stairs in boxes.

In the layering of his glass and coloured foil, Vernon was unaware of the passage of time. The seasons came and went. He laboured in rain and snow, buffeted by winds and baked by sun.

Carl was back, helping now to heave the sacks of cement and grout and wielding a hammer to break up the tiles.

One day, Vernon stumbled among the glass fragments and the boy stepped forward with startling speed and stopped him from falling. His arms had grown solid. Vernon realised that he was no longer that anxious child; his face was pale and bony but no longer pinched and narrow; it had filled out and coarsened with bristles.

"How old are you?"

"Seventeen."

Vernon was shocked; he looked down at his own wrinkled hands, the splintered yellow nails and swollen veins. "Still at school?"

"No."

"You left school?" Vernon felt he should have been consulted.

Carl shrugged and hefted a bag of tiles. "Where do you want these?"

There was a sense of urgency now about finishing the structure, now that Vernon thought he could see it complete. He imagined going up the stairs, the light growing with each step, until he was at the summit. No one, not even the ghosts of the long dead, would disturb the geometry of his thoughts. Only the coloured shafts of light would enter in to soothe his meditation.

One evening as they cleared up, Vernon was compelled to make an announcement: "It's finished," he told the boy, who was at the awkward age of never looking directly, so that Vernon had no idea whether he'd heard or gone further than even Vernon himself, down some pathway of the mind.

"What then," said the boy, "do I do now?" He was full of something, though he didn't know what it was yet; he was on the verge. He stirred pieces of brick and old rusty nails with the toe of his boot.

"It's your decision, what you do with your life," Vernon said.

No one had ever spoken to the boy about deciding. He felt as though he was standing on the edge and must jump, before he was pushed.

"Maybe a building course," suggested Vernon, "if you like the idea of being a builder."

The boy looked—a quick frightened look; their eyes, for a moment colliding.

"You OK?"

The boy didn't answer immediately. "You're getting rid of me," he said finally with something like his old whisper.

"No."

"That's what it seems like."

Vernon shrugged: "What do you want?" He drove his shovel into the earth.

"Nothing." Carl walked away, kicking at the weeds and muttering.

Vernon wondered what it was people wanted from him. As the gate clicked and the boy's footsteps died away, he heard the sound echo from the entrance to the tower and a sense of emptiness reached out to him.

*

This time Carl wouldn't go back. He'd had enough of this old man and his crazy plans. At home he lay on his bed, naked, and began to touch himself thinking of a man he'd seen in the changing rooms at the swimming pool. His penis became stiff in his hand and soon he spilled himself, except that at the last moment his mind flicked back to the great white tower he had helped to erect; the nacreous walls thrusting up in the deserted weed-grown garden.

Late the next morning, standing in the street outside Vernon's house, Carl watched for a while but there was no sign of Vernon. He went into the garden and found some boxes and a stack of old wooden scaffolding, piling them up at the foot of the tower. Then he pulled a can of lighter fuel out of his pocket. The fire was slow to catch; Carl almost stamped it out but, once the cardboard was ablaze, he stood back and warmed himself, enjoying the sense of relief and excitement as the flames took hold. Then he ran, not looking back. He'd go to a place he knew where men hunted each other for sex among the thick foliage. It was time to do this. He would find no redemption in the walls of towers, no matter how extravagantly carved.

*

Mrs Crabbe's canary fluttered in its cage and scrabbled with its claws.

"What is it?" asked Mrs Crabbe. "What's wrong with you?" She stared at the bird which stretched its wings and opened its beak in a silent gape, as though in pain. Then, abruptly, it fell from its perch.

Mrs Crabbe took up the sleek yellow body. Its eyes were half-closed, then it stiffened and hopped upright on her hand. She posted it back into its cage.

"What's that smell? It's like something burning." She wondered if she'd left the grill on and went through to the kitchenette. From there she could see Vernon's garden and the peculiar thing he was working on. A stream of smoke was pouring out of the entrance. Someone had heaped cardboard boxes against the walls. The young greedy flames flickered, reaching out for support and finding the wooden struts. From there they leapt eagerly, drawn up inside the tower by the spiralling up-draughts. The windows of coloured glass glowed before exploding in a shower of sparks.

*

Mr Kelly put down his coffee cup. It was lunch time and the playground was filling up: some children stood in knots while others careered about; as usual, there was a cluster of bodies outside the toilet block. He went back to his spreadsheet with a frown; the figures weren't adding up. Glancing up a few minutes later he thought there seemed to be fewer children; the group outside the toilet block had broken up. The spreadsheet scrolled down.

It was only after he'd finished his lunch that he noticed how silent and empty the playground was. Leaning forward and peering round to his left, he could just make out part of the playing field. The press of bodies looked like a rugby scrum. Mr Kelly reached for his scarf and headed down the corridor.

It was a windy day; the gusts caught Mr Kelly's coat tails as he hurried across the football pitch. There were now no more than a dozen or so children at the fence. They seemed to be trying to peer through the palings at what was beyond. He wondered what was on the other side of the fence. They were mostly gardens with scraps of lawn. Behind this particular bit of fence was a large pale object. Mr Kelly was surprised that he'd never noticed it before, since it was quite visible above the top of the fence.

Three girls, holding tight to each other's hands, slipped through a large hole in the fence. Mr Kelly opened his mouth to call after them, to issue orders, but the wind, strengthening still, flew into his face and he felt his cheeks pressed in with the force of the gale. He finally reached the fence and peered through the splintered panels.

The children shouted and laughed as the flames flew into the sky. It was a twisting pillar of flames that made the young faces glow and throb to a dusky red. Some of them looked round, as Mr Kelly squeezed through the fence, but most just continued to gaze at the spectacle of the white cone that was beginning to crack. The frame was showing between the empty shapes of the windows that had fallen. The flames crackled and a burst of fire shot up the centre of the frame, sucked up by the whirling gusts of wind, and the last panes of glass shattered. Thin shards of glass arced out from the exploding window. The children covered their heads and ran. Mr Kelly clapped his hand to his eye.

There was no blood, no fragment of glass; they could not find anything wrong with Mr Kelly's eyes at the hospital. They sent him home. Yet, in the days that followed, he could only sit bewildered in his office. He stared at his laptop but the lines of figures on the white screen no longer made any sense. Instead, bursts of colour bloomed behind his eyes. Each time this happened, Mr Kelly flinched. It disturbed his ordered approach to life: to be assailed by the stuff of dreams, to have things unravelling in his mind and claiming his attention when work was to be done.

"Mr Kelly?" Miss Glacer was faintly concerned, as she nibbled a Ryvita, to see that Mr Kelly was tearing small strips from a printed spreadsheet and arranging them in concentric circles on his desk.

"Yes, Miss Glacer?" Mr Kelly was smiling as he hauled himself back from the rim of something. There was a rushing sound in his ears and a taste of salt in his mouth. He could see Miss Glacer's lips moving but her words were drowned out by what he now knew to be the sound of the sea.

*

Vernon watched the tower, his refuge, disappearing in smoke and thought how nearly complete it had been. He told himself that it would be possible to rebuild. Then he thought of the back-breaking work, the wasted effort. He was afraid of the hole that was left now that there was nothing and wished that he'd never tried to mould the sand and cement. It was better gone, though the impression of it stayed with him, pressing on his eyes.

He took his shell, the pink and brown one given him by his uncle, from its place on the shelf. He caressed its familiar symmetry. He wondered how long a shell might last—hundreds of years, perhaps millions, like the skeletons of the dinosaurs. When he was a boy they'd told him to listen for the sound of the sea and he'd listened, entranced. He'd since learned that it was not the sound of the sea inside the shell, but the hollow echo of more mundane sounds.

"There's nothing now," he said to himself, looking at the grey flecks of a drizzle that was just beginning.

The shell seemed to throb before his eyes as if it was getting bigger in the fading light and he was becoming smaller.

If he closed his eyes the colours were more intense and other images came into his mind unbidden: twisting spirals that soared up into the cracked blue glaze of a winter sky, the curves and contours of a young woman's breast and the pale nipple at its summit. He found himself walking across a shiny plateau, so vast that he couldn't see the limits of it, like an ant crossing a tabletop. Then, he found himself beginning to slide as the surface of the plateau began to undulate, to draw him in.

The ugly papered walls and the dusty carpet began to fade as if these materials were just a dull layer to be peeled away. The room was getting darker still but the shell by contrast was glowing, gathering the light, and Vernon felt himself becoming a part of the continuing thread of brightness that travelled up into the pale nothingness.

Made of Glass

He'd brought his treasures, and spread them on the sun-baked concrete: purple fragments like the severed lobes of ears, others like the blanched lips of drowned sailors. Their salty taste was still in his mouth. He explored the holes that could have been nostrils with his finger, poking it into the clefts and openings.

Such a lovely lot of shells—she said as she snipped the withered roses off their stems.

I'll keep them in my box.

What box? She winced as the brown thorns caught in her woollen sleeves.

The one grandpa said he'd give me.

The old man had been in his garage. He'd let Daniel examine the grubs of screws in their canister. "Biscuits" he'd read. They were all rusty and gummed with old paint. The boy's fingers became red with the dust of old screws and sticky with cobwebs.

Crammed on the shelves were the tins of grease and the cans of oil and a cluster of rags. And there was a rack of chisels, screwdrivers and tools for poking out the eyes of small soft animals. And on a high shelf was the box of polished mahogany that once held a silver canteen of cutlery. It had a proper lock with a key and a lozenge of pale veneer on the lid.

You can have anything for your birthday, anything in the garage, said the old man with a grand gesture and, for a moment, seemed like Solomon with all his wealth.

That box, the box on the shelf there, could I have that?

Oh, I expect so. What for?

Keeping things in.

The box, Daniel told his cousin, was what he'd asked for. That box in the garage. And then he'd forgotten about it until that afternoon.

*

The boy had fallen down a flight of concrete steps and now had a plum-coloured bruise on his elbow.

My bruise... he said, going to the kitchen door.

She was grinding something in the glass jug of her mixer. The machine whizzed with such a noise, she didn't hear at first.

My bruise, look!

She touched it with hands on which the skin had grown papery and yellowed like the skin of a plucked chicken.

We'll put some butter on that nasty bruise, she said, and began to chop a piece of liver.

Daniel wondered at the butter and looked, meanwhile, at the kitchen units with their handles of marbled plastic, and the vegetables and the washing machine where she'd got her hand stuck on the spin cycle. He stared at the innocent white enamel of the machine that had tried to wrench the hand off. The thought of her blood made him feel funny, so he hobbled to the kitchen step and sat.

Why don't you go and play with your friends? she asked.

I want to stay here.

Oh, well then.

In the sitting room he stroked the cushions and watched the dust settle. On the windowsill, the skeletons of wasps crisped. In the hot afternoons the drowsy clock ticked and she sat back with her head against the antimacassar, rubbing the elbows of her cardigan into holes.

That box, said the old man coming in from being busy in the garage, I'm in a pickle. His eyes were a milky blue. I'm in a fix, you see.

The box for my birthday?

That's the one. Your cousin had asked for it before you did and I'd told him no. He says it's not fair because he asked for it first. I shouldn't have promised it to you. Now, you see, I'm in a pickle.

So Daniel gave up the box for his cousin—the birthday box of polished wood with the brass lock and key, the box to keep the shells in.

I'll remember this, said the old man. I'll remember that you got me out of a fix—and he placed his large callused hand on the boy's shoulder and the boy felt the caressing weight of it and the warmth spreading down his arm and into his chest. He felt his heart swell with pride.

The old man sat in an armchair and read a yellow newspaper that crackled and exploded when he punched the pages, then he shambled over to the TV and twizzled the knobs so that the screen glowed and flickered into life.

The shirts of the jockeys paraded jerkily through a grey rain. The old man was sitting forward in his chair, as if he was leaning along the tufted mane of the outsider who'd found his form. When the pistol exploded he was on the edge of his seat following the hurtling shapes and slapping his thighs, murmuring through gritted teeth, "Come on…"

Albert, she said, coming in and scrunching the corner

of a tea-towel, the milkman needs paying.

Outside in the garden, the rose petals fell silently in the borders like crumpled betting slips.

Just a minute, Connie, grumbled the old man because the outsider, the jockey's thighs gripping the sweating flanks, was coming up.

He's waiting, the milkman—her voice quavered into irritation.

Just hang on two ticks. The old man's shanks trembled as he stood.

The boy knelt in a corner doing something with an empty egg box.

He needs his money, do you hear, Albert? How she hated the old man's grey flannels and his white shirts.

Albert, the milkman!

For God's sake! Can't I watch the damned race?

The boy! she hissed.

Blast the lad, but he went finally, to fetch his wallet from his coat pocket.

After lunch they slept, the pair of them, mouths gaping, the soft gums and lips grown slack. The old man's nose hair quivered in his nostrils with the soft flow of air.

Under their eyelids the eyeballs twitched blindly as they moved through their dreams. The moisture glistened in the slits under the lids. Daniel visited one, then the other, peering as closely as he had examined the limpets that clung in the rock pools. He explored their slumbering forms and grew bored.

Softly, in his socks, Daniel slipped into the bedroom and approached the shrine with its silvery triptych of bevelled glass, in which his reflection was flanked with two admiring selves, three simpering smiles, three pairs of hands fluttering over the brushes and combs, the crocheted mats and the glass bowl in which a pair of pearl earrings rolled in a nest of hair grips.

He touched the forbidden objects, picking up a hair clasp in mother-of-pearl, pinning it into his hair, pulling the hair back from his round forehead.

Fumbling with the handles of the heavy oak drawers he slid open the top drawer. He began to tremble, to shake at the knees. In a case of mottled shagreen was the necklace of glass beads. Against his neck the beads scratched and settled. He put a hand up to his hair, as he'd seen her do, to settle the little comb. He seemed to swim out of the mirror towards himself, transformed momentarily, a pale shimmering creature newly cast from fragments of melted light.

Daniel moved to the other side of the bedroom and turned back to face himself. He stepped towards the mirror, gliding between the ranks of admirers, nodding first to one side and then the other. There were muted gasps. Daniel has arrived, they whispered.

As he paused and smiled, turning to observe the beads as they swung against his chest, a sudden movement in the depths of the mirror caught his attention. The old man was standing in the bedroom doorway, peering into the dimness.

What're you doing? The voice was suspicious though he couldn't yet make out what the boy was up to.

Daniel grasped at the necklace to pull it off but the

beads clung together and the necklace twisted itself in his fingers and the more he yanked at it the more it tightened.

The old man, whose eyes were still getting used to the gloom, asked again: What are you playing at in here?

The boy wrenched and the tangle of beads finally gave, the beads came apart in his hands, exploding with a soft splutter onto the flowered carpet and rattling away under the bedstead.

What is it you're doing?

The last of the beads fell with a muted chink and the boy knelt and began to scoop them up.

Leave them alone, said the grandfather in such a low whisper that the boy glanced up into his eyes. For a moment he thought the old man was smiling.

The old man let his large hands hang down helplessly. If the boy had been a piece of circuitry he could have tinkered, but the cavernous reaches of the mind repelled him.

Look at you, he said, just look at yourself.

And he restrained himself, only just, from shaking the troublesome mechanism.

Reflected in the glass was a scruffy child with a comb hanging from a tangle of hair and a lop-sided t-shirt from which a broken string of beads dangled.

The box, whispered the boy.

Box? What box?

The box, you said you wouldn't forget.

Forget? What in blazes are you talking about?

The box you said you'd give me. You said you wouldn't forget.

They looked at each other above the carpet littered with grains of light.

The old man stumped out of the room at last, his fingers twitching for a cigarette.

*

Black hooves thundered on the ceiling, beating the rhythm of blood forced through veins. Daniel's fingers fought back the covers that threatened to smother him. His cry was thin amid the thunderous hammering and yet she came, the old woman, her hair wild from being dragged out of sleep.

She tried to soothe him with a song. *Three blind mice, three blind mice*, she quavered and shook, unable to make any sense of the child. It was three thirty in the morning and he was looking at her, out of deep-set black eyes.

Then the old man came, the white tufts sticking up on his shining skull:

What is it? Has he wet the bed?

No, she said, it's not that.

Oh for pity's sake, what then? What can it be at this time of the morning?

But Daniel could not say what it was, for he was fumbling, like one of the blinded tail-less mice, through a hopeless maze.

See how they run, see how they run...

Your grandmother is very worried, said the old man putting his head in his hands.

She carried the child into her own bedroom, rocking him uncertainly in her arms. As she turned to the mirror he caught sight of himself in the glass, clinging to her quilted dressing gown with his eyes grown huge.

He's feverish, she said, perhaps he's caught a chill.

I don't know. I don't understand the boy. The old man sank onto his mattress and covered his head with a pillow.

*

In the morning sun Daniel knelt before an egg box, trickling sand into the base of each cardboard dimple. Into the sand he poked the purple eyes of flowers he'd snipped and the broken bits of shells. He was so absorbed he didn't notice the two who were watching him from their creaking garden chairs.

She wrote *cheese* and *potatoes* on her list.

We need a few things, Albert, if you wouldn't mind popping to the grocers. She threw a glance at the boy's lowered head. I'll stay with Daniel.

He needs toughening up. We shouldn't treat him as if he's made of glass. The old man pulled his battered hat forward against the sun. The chair wheezed and the boy looked up squinting into the glare.

Daniel, he said, you'll come with me to the shops.

No, he murmured making a small adjustment to a landscape.

Now there's a good chap.

No.

But Daniel was hoiked to his feet.

We're going to get you a haircut.

*

While the barber dealt with his grandfather's hair, Daniel sat on a narrow bench under the window and leafed through an old magazine. The barber seemed not to have noticed the boy and stared hard at the wrinkled skin of the old man's neck as he tucked in the cape.

Cut it short, said the old man settling himself under the billowing black.

Yes, Mr Carole.

As he clipped away at the white hair, the barber caught the boy's eye in the mirror. The grey searching glance seemed to pluck at a raw nerve in the boy, a nerve that tingled with recognition of something shared, then twitched away like the sea-anemone he'd touched in the rock pool that closed itself up tight against the probing of an alien intelligence.

Nicholas Silver, the old man was saying, now there's a horse.

He's finding his form, maybe.

They say he'll sweep the board this season.

The barber pinched an invisible hair from the old man's collar. I'd put my money on Red Alligator. He flicked up the cloth and stood back. All done, and the boy?

Cut it as short as you can; he's got nits.

The barber's cold fingers touched his collar, but briefly, to tuck in a piece of cloth, and the scissors snapped in his ears as the curls fell in his lap. The shearing scissors soothed him into a state of dullness, almost lulling him to sleep, until the blades caught the tip of his ear and made him jump. There was a tiny nick in the top of his left ear and the barber was dabbing with cotton wool. He was about to swab at it with something reeking from a jar.

No, said the old man, he doesn't want any of that stuff.

*

In the trembling depths, something stirred—a transparent

shrimp with a tiny heart of glass pulsing at its centre. It picked delicately at a grain of sand and, with a flick its tail, vanished.

As he peered into the pool, he saw himself reflected, hair cropped close. He leaned over the water, picking at the scab on his ear. The clouds behind his head moved across the disk of the sun and he saw himself more clearly still. When he breathed, the surface rippled and the scalloped edges of the clouds were shivered to pieces. He smiled at his reflection, so close now his lips almost touched. His face was framed by waving strands of weed.

Daniel! A voice called. Come here!

Figures moved in the distant haze far out on the shining sand. Someone turned a slow awkward cartwheel; another raised an arm to wave. Daniel, holding up his hand to the horizon, could pinch the wriggling body between his index finger and thumb, could have crushed the life out.

Daniel!

But he would not go, not this time. They'd only make him kneel on razor shells and kick sand in his eyes and push him down the steps. Why should he go when he was happy in his garden?

The sun broke through then and the shadows in the pool shifted from grey to turquoise. A minute pearl-grey crab edged out from beneath a stone and a ripple disturbed Daniel's features as he gazed at the reflection of the massing clouds behind his head.

Acknowledgements

Acknowledgements are due to the following editors for publishing some of the stories in this collection:

Trevor Denyer
Midnight Street Magazine
'Paper Wraps Rock', 'The Rope'

Rachel Kendall
Sein und Werden
'Anton's Discovery', 'The Island'

Sheryl Tempchin
Zahir Magazine
'Lady with an Ermine', 'Shell Fire'

Des Lewis
Nemonymous
'The Secret Life of the Panda'

Andrew Hook
New Horizons
'City in Flames'

Thanks to all the members of my writing group: Gordon Collins, Hilary Stanton, Peter Tovell, Philippa Champain, Stephanie Amey and Udara who have helped to shape many of the stories in this book.

Thanks to Quentin S. Crisp who has guided this venture with steady judgement.

And finally, thanks to Martin Hammond.

CPSIA information can be obtained at www.ICGtesting.com
Printed in the USA
LVOW061609110512

281382LV00002B/1/P

9 781907 681134